UNTETHERED

SHIFTER NIGHT

CHARLENE HARTNADY

DEDICATION

This book is dedicated to my bestie.
Your guy is out there, my friend xxx

CHAPTER 1

Ana should never have agreed to coming to a place like this. The restaurant was a hive of activity. Every single table was taken. It was the best place to go to in town, so it wasn't that big of a surprise that even the waiting area and the bar were full. Crystal glasses, linen serviettes, the whole nine yards. It wasn't easy to get a table in here. The Red Mole was normally booked at least two weeks in advance. She'd only ever eaten here once for her best friend Edith's thirtieth birthday a couple of months ago.

Ana's heart beat faster. Her hands felt a little clammy and a knot formed in her stomach. Who was she kidding? The knot had been there the whole day. It had just grown and tightened since walking in. She stopped for a second to catch her breath. Then stayed there, hand resting on the wall, for another five just to be sure.

Was this normal nervousness or... something else?

Was she about to...?

She put a hand to her belly. Her breathing remained a little elevated, but nothing out of the ordinary. *I have this.*

I do! Doctor Brenner had given her the go-ahead. It was just a stupid little date. Ana sucked in a deep breath and kept walking in the direction the hostess had pointed her. The table in the corner… to the left and…

There.

Right! Okay!

She could breathe a little easier since he looked just like his online picture. A suit, dark styled hair and a megawatt smile. Her date stood up… good god, he was tall too. In short, he was really good-looking in a neat, professional kind of way. His profile said he was an accountant, he looked like an accountant. It was a positive start. She willed her hands to stop shaking.

He stepped around the table and took a few steps towards her. "Hi, I'm Brett. You must be… Ana."

She said her name simultaneously, a nervous giggle escaped. Brett put his hand out and she shook it. His hand was soft, as was his skin. *Please don't let my hand feel sweaty. Please don't let me embarrass myself.*

Brett let go almost immediately, a smile still on his face. "It's so good to meet you. You look exactly like your picture." He gave her the once over and she could tell he liked what he saw. She had decided to go with a plain black figure-hugging dress. It came to just above the knee. Ana had taken the time to do her hair and to put on a little make-up. In short, she'd gone to a lot of trouble.

"So do you." Her voice was a little high-pitched.

"For a few minutes there, I thought you were going to stand me up." He arched a brow.

Ana smiled and shook her head. "I might be ten minutes late, but I would never not show." At least, not without telling him first. The thought of canceling had crossed her mind once or twice today.

"Here, allow me." Brett pulled a chair out for her.

"Thank you." She smiled at him as she sat down and he smiled back, taking his own seat opposite of her. So far so good. The knot in her stomach eased its hold just a smidgen and she could breathe a little easier.

The waitress came around to the table and took her order. A glass of white wine. Something light and easy, just like she hoped the evening would go.

Ana saw a tumbler of whiskey on the rocks already on the table. It was dripping with condensation. It looked like Brett had not only arrived on time but most likely, he'd arrived early. Another server came to the table with a basket of breads and a plate of different kinds of butter. "Truffle, herb and regular." He pointed at each of the creamy mounds before walking away.

"So, do you do this kind of thing regularly?" Brett asked as soon as they were alone, he leaned forward slightly in his chair.

Talk about hitting her with a difficult question right off the bat. "Um... are you talking about dating, or...?"

Brett chuckled. "Of course not, a woman like you must get asked out all the time. I'm sure you go on plenty of dates?"

Yeah... no! She smiled, hoping he wasn't expecting a reply. She couldn't tell him that this was her first date in one and a half years. She certainly couldn't tell him what a disaster her last date had been. She hadn't even made it to the one before that. *Not thinking about it!*

"I'm talking about online dating," Brett answered, not picking up on her discomfort. "Do you do this a lot?"

"This was the first time I tried online dating," she

answered simply.

The waitress arrived with her chardonnay. "Would you like some ice with that?"

Ana shook her head. "This is perfect, thanks."

"Are you ready to order your appetizers?" She held her pen poised over a pad. "The oysters are…"

"Give us a couple of minutes, please. We haven't even looked at the menus yet," Brett said, pointing at the leather-bound menus in front of them.

The waitress gave a nod. "No problem, take your time."

Ana picked up her menu. It would give her something to do with her hands which ☐ thank god ☐ had stopped shaking.

Brett drew her attention before she could open it. "Yeah, this is my first date where I had to swipe right." He smiled. "I must say, I'm glad it's not something you do all the time. I was a little worried about the kind of women I might meet through this type of service."

Ana wasn't sure what to say to that so she picked up her wine and took a sip. She gave a small nod to show that she was listening.

"Didn't you find it weird having to sift through all the profiles?"

"It *was* a little strange."

Brett picked up his menu but didn't open it. "I guess we live in a world where it's becoming more and more difficult to meet people in the regular fashion. I work twelve-hour days so…"

"I can understand how that must make it difficult."

"Yeah well, one must work hard to get ahead." He opened his menu but didn't look down. "I recently made partner at my firm." He took a sip of his whiskey.

"Oh, that's great. Congratulations!"

"Just last month and four years early."

Ana frowned. "Four years?"

"Yup, I had planned to make partner by forty. I'm only thirty-six so that's sooner than I'd anticipated."

"It certainly is. That's wonderful. You must be thrilled."

"I am." He looked serious for a moment, his brow creased and his lips pursed. "I have a four-bedroom home, with a pool and a big landscaped garden."

"Oh!" If he thought to impress her with money, he was sadly mistaken. "That's great!"

"Complete with a white picket fence." He swirled his glass. "Granite tops in the kitchen and marble finishes in all the bathrooms. It's quite lovely."

She nodded, taking another sip of her wine. "That's wonderful."

"All that's missing is a family." He was looking at her strangely, almost like he was judging her reaction. Maybe a guy like him had women coming onto him for his money.

Ana put down her glass, giving another nod. Maybe he just liked the attention that money brought him. Well, he was barking up the wrong tree. She scanned through the appetizers, a couple of things catching her eye.

"What do you do?" Brett picked up his own menu and opened it, he kept his eyes on her.

"I'm a nurse at the Sweetwater Hospital."

"Oh!" He smiled. "How nice!" The way he said it was kind of patronizing.

"I really enjoy my work, I've—"

"I guess being a medical worker is something that could come in handy." He rubbed his chin.

Ana frowned. "What do you mean?"

"In the home, that is. I'm sure you want to become a mother… have kids one day. Maybe even sooner rather than later?" He raised both brows.

"Yes." Her heart beat a little faster. "I would love to be a mom… one day that is." Her chest tightened. Ana picked up her glass and took a big glug of wine, not sure where this conversation was going. Not liking the direction.

"Shall I order some water?" He frowned, glancing at the wine glass still in her hand. He had a look of disapproval but she knew she must be reading him wrong.

"Yes, that would be nice," she answered, trying to be polite. Ana put the wine glass back down.

He settled back in his chair and smiled at her. "It's good to know."

"What is?" she asked, as Brett flagged down one of the waiters and ordered water.

"Good to know that you want to be a mom." He turned back to her. "It's important to establish these things early."

What was he on about? He must have seen her confused look because he elaborated. "I'm looking for marriage and a family."

Ana took another big sip of her wine, her heart all a-flutter. Her stomach knotting back up. "This… um… this is our first date. It's too soon to—"

"It's never too soon to make your intentions known," he interrupted. "I'm looking for a wife… there, it's out. I know that most women want marriage and security so I doubt I'll have much trouble. I just don't want to waste my time, is all. I realize that not everyone is looking for the same thing. Not everyone wants kids." He paused. It was like he was waiting for her to interject if she had something to say. "That's why I was a bit worried about using a dating app. I'd heard that the people you meet... the type of person... some of them are just out for a good time..." He pulled a face. "Hey, are you okay? You look a little flustered."

"I'm fine." She tried to control her breathing. *I can handle this. I can!*

Brett gave a small nod. "So, you're not just here for sex, are you?"

"No," she blurted. "Not at all." *It's fine! It's all good.*

"Well, then we can relax and enjoy our date." He narrowed his eyes, leaning forward in his seat. "Are you sure you're okay?"

Ana gasped for air, her throat closing quickly. *Please no! No!*

"Can I pour you some water?"

Ana nodded. She was way beyond water. Way beyond trying to talk. *Shit! This isn't happening. It isn't!* The room was hot... that's why she felt flushed. That's why she couldn't breathe. *Damn! Dammit all to hell!*

Brett hurriedly poured water, some of it sloshed over the rim of the glass, his eyes were filled with concern. "You're sweating."

Gee, I hadn't noticed.

She grabbed the glass and tried to drink some but it gushed over her lips and down her neck. *Cold!* Ana swallowed the little bit she could. It felt like a rock trying to go down a straw. Her throat was officially closed. The room was both spinning and crystal clear, all at the same time.

Around them, waiters carried beautifully prepared

meals and expensive bottles of wine. Diners chatted, drank and ate their meals, oblivious to the turmoil in the far corner of the room.

"What can I do?" Brett was out of his seat. "Are you having an allergic reaction? Do you have medication in your purse?" He lifted her purse from the chair next to her. "Is it in here? Try to breathe slower."

Gee, why hadn't I thought of that?

Ana realized that she was being a bitch but couldn't help it. She needed to get the hell out of there. She pushed her chair back, eliciting a hard scraping noise on the gleaming wooden floor. *Oh shit!* Now the people from the table next to them were gaping at her and one of the servers was making her way over, eyes wide.

Out!

Now!

She had to leave. If she made it outside and to the safety of her car she would be okay. It was a pity, but she didn't feel like that was going to happen. She was beginning to feel light-headed. Her stomach seemed to clamp and unclamp. Stars were beginning to flicker in and out of her vision. She felt dizzy… no, she felt… ill. Her legs might not work anymore but she needed to try.

"Out," she managed to somehow moan the word. She planted her hands on the table and used it to leverage herself up into a standing position. Well sort of. She was hunched over the table. Her glass of water tipped over, clanging as it hit, water soaked into the beautifully crisp white tablecloth.

"Ana," Brett kept calling her name. He clasped her elbow tightly. "Sit. You shouldn't be—"

Ana twisted around, trying to push past him… trying hard not to… her stomach gave a heave and out it came.

The apple she'd munched on before coming here and the wine, her vomit was sour… it was disgusting and it was all over Brett's shoes, all over his left leg. He let go of her, taking a frantic step back. Then everything went black as she passed out.

CHAPTER 2

A sh put his nose into the air and sniffed deeply. His already pointed snout elongated even more. His nostrils widened. He sniffed again, lumbering from one side of the clearing to the other, eyes shifting from left to right. His heavy fur bristled. The big male rose onto his muscular hind legs and gave another exaggerated sniff. The sound of his snuffling filled the clearing. The rest of the sounds of the forest seemed to become drowned out.

Winston could see that the male was agitated. He growled, landing heavily onto all fours before walking back to the spot he had just vacated. Winston sniffed the air as well and got... the edge of something... maybe... he ultimately got nothing. Crisp air, the scent of the nearby river. He could smell the earth, a squirrel that had recently run across this particular patch of earth. He could scent the daisies growing on a patch of moss nearby.

He could scent many other things as well that were of little importance. What had gotten his friend so rattled?

He watched as Ash ripped up the earth with his heavily clawed paws, frequently stopping to sniff some more. Then there was the familiar sound of bones cracking, of tendons reshaping.

Ash's low bear growl became less animal and more human... straddling the line between the two. He crouched down, fingers sinking into the earth. His body covered in a thin sheen of sweat. Ash looked his way and gave a quick lift of the chin.

It seemed his buddy wanted to have a little chat. Winston pictured his human form, feeling his wolf retract, starting with his fur. It pulled into his skin, his limbs folding in on themselves. It hurt but it was a good kind of pain. "What is it?" he said, as soon as he was shifted enough to talk. His voice still held a guttural edge, his vocal cords still remembering those of his wolf.

"Not sure." Ash was still agitated. "Something... and yet, I can't put my claw on what exactly."

Winston chuckled. "It's a known fact that wolves have a better sense of smell than bears. I didn't pick up a thing."

Ash sniffed again, even though there was no way he would pick anything up in his human form, despite the fact that his sense of smell was far superior to any mere human.

Winston chuckled at the male. Ash was his best friend. Even though they were different kinds of shifters. Even though Ash was older and an alpha. It didn't matter in the least. They had still become fast friends from the word go. "Let's change back and head home," he suggested.

Human skin or not, Ash bristled, the male still on high-alert. "Call it a gut feeling... something isn't right."

Winston paced to where Ash was standing.

The male seemed to be listening for something, his brow heavily furrowed. "I wish I knew what the fuck was going on."

"Something is definitely up. Herds of game don't disappear into thin air. At this point though you're just hungry. We're all hungry… for meat."

Ash's nostrils flared, his eyes were focused on the canopy up ahead. "I'm hungry but that's not it. Something spooked the game. I sensed something out here. Something's wrong!"

Winston shook his head. "If there was something in these woods, we'd know about it."

"Make no mistake," Ash paused. "There is something in these woods. With thousands of square miles, it would be easy for them to hide."

"From us? We're shifters for fuck's sake. They can't hide from us." Winston shook his head. "Now that's crazy talk."

Ash shrugged. "You're probably right but I'd still be willing to bet my right nut on it."

Winston laughed. "You're on. I'm sure it's a simple case of the herds migrating though. Something to do with the solar system and the way the planets are aligned. Or maybe global warming. It's fucking with nature in the worst of ways."

The big male shrugged, his agitation from earlier all but gone. "What happened to you on Saturday?"

"What do you mean, what happened to me?" Winston folded his arms. "Nothing happened."

"You're right, nothing happened," Ash chuckled.

Winston fought an eye roll and lost. *Here we go again.*

"You took a female back to your hotel room but didn't

touch her." Ash grinned. "My sources tell me she was not too thrilled when she left. Made a ton of noise and called you a limp dick." Ash choked out a laugh. "Limp dick," he muttered to himself, still laughing.

Winston rolled his eyes a second time. "Yeah, yeah, it's 'Pick on Winston' week. Why can't a male just change his mind? Why was it that my dick immediately got a bad rep? Why can't a male walk away from sex without being ridiculed?"

"There was nothing wrong with that female." Ash shook his head. "Trent told me it was the blonde with the hair all the way to her ass. She's a little noisy, but—"

"My point exactly." Winston blew out a breath.

"Are you still banging on about how you've had it with fucking around?"

"You have no idea." Winston narrowed his eyes. "You've only been at it for a couple of years."

Ash's eyes darkened, pain caused his features to pinch.

"Hey, bro…" Winston kept his voice soft. "I'm sorry. That was out of line." *What the fuck is wrong with me?*

Ash shook his head. "Nah!" He rolled his shoulders. "I'm fine. Don't worry about it."

Winston could see that he wasn't. What male would be?

"So, no more Shifter Night for you then? No more going to the 'Dark Horse'? No more females? No more fun… fuck! I'm glad I'm not you."

"Who says I can't still go to Shifter Night? Who says I can't spend time with the females? Who says that sex equates to the only form of fun to be had?"

Ash barked out a laugh. It was deep and throaty. "You have got to be fucking kidding me. You still plan on hitting town?"

"Sure," Winston shrugged, "why not? I don't plan on fucking around but I can still go and enjoy myself."

"We're meat to those human females, plain and simple. Meat. They don't want us for anything other than our dicks," Ash palmed his cock as he said it.

"You're wrong. Humans want nothing more than to spend more time with us. I've had numerous females beg me to meet with them again, or to take them back with me. They *wanted* a relationship with me. Begged me for a chance."

"They wanted more cock. It's always about the sex, trust me. They don't want to take you home to meet daddy. They don't want you to take them out to dinner or to go dancing. They want you because they know you have a big dick and you know how to use it. That's it, end of story."

"Cynical much?"

"Nope." Completely deadpan.

Winston shrugged. "I guess I'm just better relationship material. Females definitely want me for more than just sex."

"How do you figure?" Ash narrowed his eyes.

"I'm better looking and I'm easier to talk to."

Ash choked out a laugh. "So full of shit."

Winston grinned. "You know it's true."

"I'm better in the sack. The other stuff means fuck all to me," said in true Ash style.

Winston nodded. "Yeah well, I'm sick of being used. Sick of using females right back. I guess I want more, that's all."

"Said like a true pussy."

"Who the fuck are you calling a pussy?" he growled.

"Pussy wolf," Ash lowered his voice. His canines were longer than they had been a few seconds ago.

"Fuck you, bear." He felt his own teeth erupt, his hairs stood up and his muscles bunched.

"Plenty of fucking for me; for you," he laughed, the sound rough and raw, "not so much." Hair sprouted from his chest. His jaw elongated.

"Fucking around! Huh!" Winston felt his own fur begin to sprout. He felt the cords in his throat tighten. "It's meaningless, emotionless and not for me. Not anymore." So deep he could barely understand himself. "I want something more."

Ash changed back. The male breathed deeply, even hunched over the middle. It took effort to shift. He pulled himself upright, eyes on Winston. "Something more." He was breathing deeply, his eyes on the ground. "You don't want love… trust me on that. Love can destroy a male." His friend took in a deep breath and shifted.

It was exactly what Winston wanted. It was what he craved.

CHAPTER 3

"What an asshole," her doctor announced.

"To be fair, I did puke on him." Ana still felt appalled at what had gone down.

"Still." Doctor Brenner shook her head, looking shocked. "He just left, without making sure that you were okay first?" She cocked her head. "That's just plain wrong. Maybe you were having an allergic reaction, or maybe you were," she made a noise that gave away her exasperation, "I don't know… diabetic and going into shock. He simply left. What an ass. I say good bloody riddance."

"I'm not diabetic and I certainly wasn't having an allergic reaction. Maybe he was right to throw down that fifty and hightail it out of there. At least, that's what the staff told me had happened once I came to." She felt her cheeks heat at the memory. "I woke up a few minutes later on the floor of the manager's office. I was in the recovery position with a wet towel around my forehead." She felt her cheeks heat just thinking about it.

"Oh good!" Doctor Brenner's eyes shone with

concern. "At least there are some good folks in this world."

"You don't understand." She covered her eyes with her hand for a moment. "The manager was on the phone with 911 at the time… yep… the emergency services."

"No!" Her therapist drew out the word, then she chewed down on her bottom lip to stifle a laugh. "I'm sorry," she said. "That's terrible. What did you say?"

"I told them I was fine… because I *was* fine. They wouldn't believe me at first but I managed to convince them that I'd fainted. They made me promise to go to the emergency room. I feel like such a failure." Ana felt her eyes fill with tears. "I'm never going to get over what happened."

"You're not a failure," Doctor Brenner said the words with such conviction that for a moment she was tempted to believe them. How could she though?

"Didn't you hear me, doc? I puked all over him."

"Who says they want marriage and a family on the first date? I'm surprised he didn't propose. I might have reacted in much the same way." She rolled her eyes. "If you don't mind me saying, that guy sounds a bit strange. You shouldn't be so hard on yourself."

"Brett's just an analytical type personality through and through, the guy knows exactly what he wants. I can't blame him, he was just being honest." She sighed.

"He was a bit of a jerk though… he sounded like a jerk to me. I'm surprised he didn't make you fill out a questionnaire before he let you sit down."

Ana sniffed back her tears and smiled. "I suppose he was a bit of a weirdo. I wouldn't put a questionnaire past a guy like him. He probably saved that for the second date."

Her therapist looked at her pointedly. "This was a tiny hiccup. You're making huge progress, the last date you went on you had an attack as soon as the guy introduced himself to you and you didn't even manage to get out of your car on the one before that. I think you would've been fine with this Brett guy if he hadn't mentioned the M-word."

It was true. Ana had felt pretty okay until that moment. Why did he have to mention marriage? Why did he ask her if she wanted children? "You might be right. I can't risk it though. I just wish there was some sure-fire way to... to get better." She felt bad saying it. *Move on... get over it...* It felt too much like forgetting her past. Forgetting someone who had meant everything to her and a time in her life that she had never been happier.

Doctor Brenner looked deep in thought for a few moments. "What about role-playing?"

Ana felt herself frown. "Role-playing?" she repeated, hearing the skepticism in her voice.

"Role-playing. Don't you have a really good male friend or maybe a colleague? Go out on a couple of fake dates – go through the motions. It's a proven fact that desensitizing works on patients suffering from phobias."

"It's not like I'm afraid of snakes... or heights. It's not that simple."

"It is though. Your fear works in much the same way as someone else's fear of snakes. Dating, and particularly the thought of a relationship, triggers your panic attacks. Sure, there's more to it but I really feel you would benefit from some fake dating, if you will. So, do you have a male friend or two you could enlist?"

Ana shook her head. "Carl has a girlfriend – it would be wrong to ask. Pete and I have been friends since we were kids, he's more of a brother." She shrugged. "We've been out tons of times… I'm very comfortable with him. My friend Edith has a younger brother, but…" she pulled a face. "That's eeww… he's six years my junior."

"It wouldn't be for real though."

"Still," Ana said. "I can't. He has pimples and still lives at home with his parents."

"Yikes, okay, I understand." Her therapist closed the file on her desk. "We need to try to come up with something though. A friend of a friend then… Something casual and relaxed. You need to go through the motions." She pushed out a breath. "You need to have some fun but without any real date pressure. The fun part is the most important. In fact, I prescribe it." She pulled out a pad and wrote on it, signing the bottom before handing it to Ana.

She took the paper and laughed. "That's the strangest prescription ever."

Written in the middle of the page were two words.

Have fun!

Her doctor turned serious. "It's what you need, Ana. You need to give yourself permission to have fun and in so doing, to ultimately move on."

"I want to…" her voice was thin. Her throat suddenly hurt because of the choking feeling resulting from all of the emotions inside of her. She meant it. For years now, she wished it could happen. Unfortunately, she was beginning to think it might be impossible.

CHAPTER 4

THREE WEEKS LATER...

"Come on." Edith did a twirl, it reminded her of how a half-drunken ballerina might look. This despite her best friend only having had one glass of wine. "It's Saturday night. Just say 'yes,' it isn't that difficult. It's a three letter word, for goodness sake. Three little letters." She picked up the bottle of wine off the counter and skipped back.

Her apartment was tiny so it only took three little skips. Edith sloshed some wine into Ana's glass. "I don't know... it seems like too big a step all at once."

"Your doctor ordered you to have some fun. She *ordered* you," Edith said with conviction. She tipped more wine into Ana's glass, filling it right to the rim.

"No," Ana shook her head. "She *prescribed* fun. It wasn't an order."

"Same difference. Let's just go. It will be fun. I promise. These guys are not looking for love or anything. They're here to let off steam. They're in town to have a little fun, which is exactly what the doctor ordered. Exactly what *your* doctor ordered."

Ana took a sip of her wine. "What if I have an attack?"

"What if you don't?" Edith giggled. She had a headful of curly hair. "What if you end up having more fun than you ever thought possible?"

"I don't know." Ana could hear the uncertainty in her voice. "I don't want to puke on someone again. You have no idea what it feels like."

"I've puked on someone before." Edith widened her eyes.

Ana choked out a laugh. "Somehow, I can believe that."

Edith laughed as well. "I was fifteen. My parents decided that I was old enough to babysit my younger bro. Well, epic fail... I found their stash of vodka and ended up vomiting on my dad when my parents got home."

"No way!" Ana laughed so hard that her belly hurt.

"At least, that's what they told me in the morning when I woke up feeling like there was a hole in my head and a sewer in my mouth."

Ana laughed some more. "I'm having fun right now," she blurted. "We're having fun. We don't have to go to some stupid bar."

"No, we don't." Edith plopped herself down next to her, suddenly looking serious. "I'm happy right here, if you are? Only, I don't think you are, Ana, not really. I know you want to be able to date again, I know you're lonely... that you want to meet someone, maybe settle down again one day."

Ana shook her head. "Forget settling down. I don't want to think that far ahead. I'm nowhere near ready for that." She sighed. "But, I would love to go on a date. Not just the start of a date but a whole damned date. From beginning to end." She made a groaning noise. "Sex… now there's a concept… What I wouldn't give for an orgasm. One I didn't have to give myself that is."

"It isn't the same, is it?"

"Not even close." Ana sighed.

Edith turned to face her. "You can have it all – the sexiest guys you've ever seen. I'm talking off the charts, pick your tongue up off the floor hot."

"Aren't they big and hairy? I heard they smell musky." Ana wrinkled her nose.

Edith shook her head. "Shifters don't have any body hair but they sure are big – you were right on that one." She bobbed her eyebrows. "I'm not sure about the musky smell. Honestly though," she choked out a laugh. "I'm willing to breathe through my mouth if it means being with one. They're supposed to be really fantastic in bed."

Ana giggled along with her friend.

"Let's just go." Edith sprang to her feet. "If you have an attack, we'll leave." She picked up her glass and took a sip.

"I hate having them. That's what I meant when I asked you earlier if you knew what it felt like. I was talking about having an attack, not puking on someone. It's scary. So incredibly scary. I always feel like I can't breathe. Like the room is closing in. Worst of all, I hate the way people look at me. I hate the lack of control. There is nothing I can do to stop it."

Edith put her glass down and sat on the chair next to Ana. She slid an arm around her shoulder. "I'm sorry! I didn't mean to push. I meant it when I said I was happy right here."

Ana sucked in a deep breath. She hoped to god she didn't come to regret this. "No!" her voice sounded stronger than she felt. "I think we should go. I have to keep trying. I'll never get better if I hide out at home. I can't give up."

"That's my girl." Edith jumped up and gave another twirl.

"You said these guys aren't looking for a relationship?" Some unease set in.

"Not at all! They're not allowed to date or have relationships. They come into town for sex. Straight up, all night, blow-your-mind sex."

Ana huffed out a pent up breath. "Okay then. Let's do this."

Edith gave a squeal. "Now to get you all sexied up."

Oh God, please don't let this be a mistake! Ana meant it though, she had to try. She couldn't give up.

A piece of meat.

That was how Winston felt at that moment, as well as whenever he came into town on any Saturday. On Shifter Night, as the locals had dubbed it. He felt like a piece of meat on a butcher's block, reduced to sinew, muscle and bone. *Don't forget the bone.* That was the part the human females were most interested in.

Ash had been right on the money on that note. He yelped as a hand closed over one of his butt cheeks and squeezed. Winston turned. The woman was a little older but still in great shape. She looked him up and down like he was the last piece of candy in the jar, even giving her lips a languid lick. "Hey tiger," she murmured, stepping in closer.

Nope! He wasn't feeling it. Not for her, or for the redhead earlier. He hadn't felt it for the brunette ten minutes before that either. Females approached him left, right and center. The moment he managed to lose one, another would pop up. Some were sexy, some were more girl-next-doorsy, but none held any appeal for him. Not like they used to, at any rate.

The female reached out. *No damned way!* Her hand reached further and further forward, aiming for his crotch. He sealed a hand over hers just as she was about to squeeze his dick, feeling her perfectly manicured, red nails against his palm. "I don't think so."

She smiled. "That's why you're here, isn't it?" Another glide of that tongue.

"I'm here for a drink."

"Sure." She narrowed her eyes. It was clear that she didn't believe him.

"Can I buy you a drink? We can talk." This female must have a story; one he wouldn't mind hearing.

"We can talk after." She bobbed her brows suggestively.

Yeah right! There would be no talking after. She'd be wrung out, barely capable of walking, let alone coherent speech. It wasn't that he was arrogant, it was just a simple fact. Winston shrugged. "I'm headed to the bar. You're welcome to join me."

"One drink and then we'll head out?" She raised her brows suggestively.

Meat… that's all he was to them. The shifters had somewhat of a reputation though. It was their own fault for starting Shifter Night in the first place. This was all about sex… no holds barred, all night long rutting. No emotions, no tomorrow, no future. It was about cleaning out the old pipes and giving the female as much pleasure as possible, and for years he'd been okay with that.

Make that, he'd loved it. Looked forward to it. He counted down the weeks, days and hours until it was his turn to hit Sweetwater. As of late though, it had grown old. All of it. Females didn't come to the 'Dark Horse' for the riveting conversation. They didn't see any of the shifters as anything more than meat and bone. He may as well be a giant dildo. To think he'd believed they might see something more in him. He hated to admit it, but Ash had been right.

"On second thought…" He smiled at her, watching as her eyes lit up. She was about to be bitterly disappointed. "I think I'll head out," he continued.

The glint became a spark. Oh hell, she was reading this all wrong. "On my own." He added. "Have a good evening." Winston gave a nod to the pouting human and headed out.

"Hey!" Ash yelled. "Going so soon?" The bear alpha grinned and a couple of human females swooned.

"I'll see you tomorrow," Winston said, hand on the door.

Ash laughed, he mouthed the word 'pussy,' putting his arm around a curvy blonde. Winston couldn't help but chuckle. Just then, two females came through the door. He stood to the side. The one female had a head of curly hair. She eyed him like he was… a piece of meat. The other female looked shell-shocked. Like she didn't really want to be there. Her eyes were wide and really blue. The female was so nervous, she didn't even see him standing there.

"Ladies." He tipped his head, leaving the bar, the noise, all of the hustle and bustle behind him.

CHAPTER 5

B ig, built and really cute, he ticked all the boxes. Every last one. Why, then, was she shivering inside the bathroom? Too afraid to come out? What was wrong with her? Nothing. Everything. No, she was an idiot and a complete prude, and in that order. No she wasn't, there were real reasons why this was so hard for her. She needed to cut herself some slack.

"Have a one-night stand," Edith had said. "You'll love it," she had whispered behind her hand. "You need it." Then she'd gone on to scrunch up her nose and look at her like she was a lost cause. No matter the prodding for Ana to do this though, Edith had still made it very clear that she was not guaranteed success. None of them were. If you managed to snag one of them, you were lucky. "If only it was guaranteed," she'd said. Apparently, if Ana could get it right, it'd be the best night of her life. If that was so true, why were her hands shaking and her heart racing? Why did she feel ill? In the end, she knew exactly why, only she didn't want to think about it right at that moment. She had come a long way. She could do this.

Ana hadn't puked on him and she could still breathe. It was all good. She could still do this. She had to. Sex with another human being. Good sex, if Edith was to be believed, and somehow she knew it was true. The guy in the next room was a dream come true.

Her stomach clenched again, this time accompanied by a tightening feeling. Here she was, catch of the century waiting in the hotel bed, and she wanted to run away.

A knock sounded on the door and she almost jumped right out of her skin.

"You okay?" he sounded concerned. So, this guy was big, built, cute *and* sweet? A real catch. It didn't matter because she still felt sick though.

"Fine." Her voice didn't sound fine. "I'm coming."

There was a chuckle followed by. "Not yet you aren't." More chuckling. "But you will be soon." Low and deep. The way he said it should have had her toes curling. Instead, her stomach gave another lurch.

"Okay," she said, trying a bit harder to sound normal. When she wasn't normal. A normal woman would be loving the hell out of this. A normal woman would be in that bed having the best sex of her life by now. A normal woman would not have said an idiot thing like 'okay' to a statement like that.

Hearing him say that should have had her running out with her arms outstretched. Instead, her stomach gave another lurch.

She could totally leave and blow him off but the thing was, no matter how sick she felt, she had put a lot of work into this night. She was wearing matching underwear. Not only that, it was a new set. The one she had bought months ago but had never worn. It was sexy and red and looked so darned good on her. Also, she'd done her hair and her nails, shaved her legs and her underarms. She'd even gone so far as to wax. The pain had been excruciating but worth it. Her girl bits had never looked so good. She had never looked so good – and yet here she was, hiding. Still fully clothed and shivering like a scaredy cat.

The plan had been to brush her teeth and to take off the dress so that she could present herself in just the underwear and heels. Her breathing picked up, together with her heart rate at the thought of walking out of there half-naked. Her throat felt dry as a bone in the desert. No, drier. Going out there in her undies was not going to happen.

No way.

Ana swallowed hard. Even her hands felt clammy. She could do this. She just needed to go out there and look at him again. Once she got an eyeful, she'd be revving on all cylinders, she just knew it. Okay, she hoped that's what would happen.

Before she could give herself a chance to overthink it, Ana pushed the door open and strode out into the hotel room like she owned it. "Fake it till you make it," her granny had always said, and it was as good advice as any.

He was stretched out on the bed. For the life of her, she couldn't remember his name. Ana had always had this little problem, she forgot things when she was nervous. What's-his-name had ditched his shirt and was all long limbs and huge muscles. He grinned. With blond hair, the bluest of eyes and dimples from here until next Tuesday, he was the epitome of hot. Yet, all she felt was the slow rolling of her stomach, followed by a hard clench when he tapped his denim-clad lap. What's-his-name wanted her to straddle him.

No.

No.

No.

There would be no straddling. No sex. No orgasms. What the hell had possessed her to even try this? Oh yes, the fact that she hadn't had sex in a couple of years. Ever since… Her heart gave a clench and her stupid lip quivered.

"Are you okay?" He frowned and sat up. "You don't look well." He sniffed the air. "You do not need to feel nervous. I'm going to take good care of you, I promise."

"I know that, it's just…" She clasped and unclasped her hands. "I made a mistake coming here. I was so sure I could do this." She mumbled to herself, "I'm so stup – "

"Let's chill for a bit… have a bite to eat, or – "

Ana shook her head. "I guess I'm just not cut out for the whole 'jump in bed with someone you don't know' thing. I've never done this before and…" She stopped herself from babbling any more. "I'm so sorry…" Cody! His name was Cody. "Cody, I just can't."

"Okay, no problem." He got up off the bed and she had to crane her head to keep eye contact.

What the hell was wrong with her? It had been years. Years! Surely she could move on. Just thinking it though made guilt flood her.

"You are a lovely female. I only wish it was my name on the list this time round, we may have been able to get to know one another… I'm not talking just sexually, I'm talking from a relationship point of view." *List? What list?* The word relationship registered and she started to really feel panicky. It was like the walls were closing in. Her throat felt tight. It was about to happen. *Oh flip!*

Out.

Now.

"Okay, Cody," she blurted. "I'm going to go now."

He nodded. Ana turned on her heel and left. Thankfully the door wasn't locked. Once outside the room, she put her back to the wood and pushed out a ragged breath. Normally taking a couple of deep breaths helped, but not today. Not even a little bit. She needed to get the hell out of there.

Ana started to jog down the walkway. She would head for the parking lot and call a cab once she got there. Despite being outside, her chest still felt tight, her throat as well. *Air! Need air!*

One second she was jogging and the next, she was colliding with a wall. Hard and unyielding. The little bit of air she had was pushed out of her lungs and all at once. Something gripped her arms. Come to think of it, the wall was warm.

"Easy," a deep, rich voice. "Are you alright?" Then he was peeling her off of his chest and looking her over, concern reflected in his eyes. They were big and brown. A light buttery brown. Very beautiful. His hair was a little overgrown and sandy blond.

He was huge, way bigger than Cody. Broad shoulders and thick arms. One of *them* then.

Her head spun a bit. Must be from all the adrenaline, she thought. That, together with the panic and lack of oxygen, even though her chest was heaving. Although he seemed sweet enough, she still felt the need to get away and to do it now. "I'm fine," she half-yelled, trying to pull free.

"Hey." He frowned. "You're safe. I've got you." His voice was just as beautiful as he was.

It helped to calm her some. This had been such a bad idea. Such a seriously dumb thing to have done. She should have known better. "I must go." Still laced with some panic. Okay a lot of panic. She could feel that her eyes were wide. "I don't want this… to be here. I'm not interested in any type of one-night stand and I don't want a relationship. I just want to go home." She said it in a rush of words that tumbled out even though he hadn't asked for any type of explanation. Even though he hadn't made any kind of demand.

"I understand." Still the same calm tone. "That's perfectly fine. I'm not looking for a hook-up and I'm not on the list, so no relationship for me either. I was out for some air. I think," he narrowed his eyes, seeming to look right through her, "you could use some too."

That's when she realized how fast she was breathing. It was worse than before. At this rate, she was going to hyperventilate.

CHAPTER 6

The human's eyes were wide. They reminded him of the full moon at midnight. Only, not nearly as calm. Tension radiated off of her in waves. Her hair was a wild tangle. A better reflection of her mood. Her face was pale. She was like a deer that had caught scent of a predator. He recognized her from earlier at the bar. The shell-shocked one. He wasn't surprised to see her running. Not everyone was cut out for Shifter Night. "Did something happen?" he asked, releasing his hold on her somewhat. She'd looked nervous before but not like this. Had one of the males tried something? Why was she running scared like this?

"No!" She shook her head. "Nothing! Unless being an idiot counts." She sighed.

"Are you sure nothing happened? Did anyone try something? Did…"

The skittish human pursed her lips for a moment. "No, really. Nothing happened. I overreacted. I'm… a lost cause, okay?" She was panting heavily, liked she'd just run a couple of miles.

"I'm going to let you go now, please don't run away."
She nodded.

Winston released his hold on her completely and took a step back. She was still breathing too quickly, still far too pale but better than before. "Would you like to go for a walk?"

She shook her head, her eyes widened back up to full moon status.

"Okay, okay." He put up his hands, tempted to back up even more. Even more tempted to look at the ground, anything to keep from spooking her. "Do you see that bench over there?" He pointed to a wooden seat between rooms eighteen and nineteen. It overlooked the garden.

She gave a tentative nod. Winston noticed how her legs were bent at the knee, how her leading leg was just that inch or two more forward than the other. She was getting ready to run for it.

"How's about we sit there for a few minutes, seeing as we both need some air? I'm a shifter."

"I know. I mean, I realized," she spoke quickly.

"Well, that means you're safe with me. Firstly, because I would never hurt you – shifters are creatures of great honor – and secondly, because I wouldn't allow harm to befall you."

She pushed out a big lungful of air and gave a nod. He noticed how she looked down at her feet, how her shoulders sagged.

Winston took the first step towards the bench and the little female followed. She sat as far on the other side as she could get. He did the same, still careful not to spook her.

They sat in silence for a time. It was a peaceful time of the day. The odd car could be heard in the distance, or the barking of a dog. Winston preferred very early morning though. That time just before the sun rose. It was normally crisp and extremely quiet. The time just before the rest of the world awoke. Or, at least, that's what it felt like to him. Especially back home. Deep in the mountains, surrounded by miles and miles of trees.

"I'm sorry!" she whispered.

"No need."

"It's just that I… made a mistake… I made a really stupid mistake. I shouldn't have come. I'm sorry to have interrupted your night." She sucked in a quick breath. "Oh flip! I'm sure you have somewhere to be… someone waiting for you or," she groaned, "you came out here in the hopes of having a quiet cigarette after… after… you know." She looked horrified for a few seconds. "I'm sorry… I'll just…" She stood up.

"Sit." He chuckled. Couldn't help himself. "Please. You're wrong on all of those counts."

"Oh! Okay, so whoever you were with left already. Okay then." She breathed out, touching a hand to her chest. "Makes me feel marginally better." Thankfully, she sat back down.

"Nah!" He shook his head. "No worries. You have that wrong too."

The female frowned. "Aren't you a shifter?" Her frown deepened. "Of course you are, you just said so. It's Shifter Night."

Winston smiled. "Yeah, I know. I'm not looking to hook up though."

"Said no shifter male ever, or so I have been told…" He could see her thinking it over. "Did I misunderstand what Shifter Night is all about? I was just at the Dark Horse and I'm sure I didn't misunderstand. Maybe

Shifter Night isn't Shifter Night for all shifters then?"

"You didn't misunderstand. The guys all come through to unwind. I just decided I didn't feel like it this time."

"I don't have much experience with shifters. It's just that I heard they all wanted to hook up. I'm—"

He laughed. "Don't worry about it."

"Sorry, I'm nervous, I babble when I'm nervous. Ignore me." Her breathing had normalized. Her eyes had lost that frightened look.

"I'm Winston." He held out his hand.

Her heart rate picked up a tad and she looked down at his hand like it was scaly or bleeding or something.

"I won't bite you." Maybe not the best thing to say to such a timid female but he said it anyway.

The female giggled. "Right, well, um…" She took his hand in a surprising grip and shook once before letting go. Then she stared off into the night sky. She was a pretty, little thing. Sandy brown hair with blonde streaks and blue eyes. Her hair smelled funny, like she'd put too many products in it. *Why did human females do such things?* It was beyond him. They were perfectly beautiful without all the bleaching, varnishing, and primping.

Take this female for example. Her lips were full. She didn't need the lipstick or gloss. She wasn't quite as curvy as human females often were but she was gorgeous nonetheless. Plump little breasts and a tight little ass. He immediately felt guilty for checking her out. It had become normal to size up the opposite sex. To pick and choose who he wanted to spend Shifter Night with. It was wrong when he thought about it. They were just as much meat to the shifters as the shifters were to them. Plain wrong and it wasn't going to happen again.

"This is the part where you tell me your name," Winston said.

"Oh!" A gasp. "I'm Ana."

"It's good to meet you." He paused for a time. "You're sure nothing happened that I should know about? I can help, you know?"

"No." She shook her head. Her cheeks heated. "Cody was a perfect gentleman. I just... I get these panic attacks." She glanced his way, then quickly averted her eyes. "They used to be really bad. I've worked hard at getting them... myself under control." She swallowed hard. "I thought I had a handle on it but I guess I don't. Like I said, I'm a lost cause."

She sounded so sad, looked sad come to think of it. "Don't say that," Winston said. He wanted to reach out and touch her arm but he thought better of it. Didn't want to scare her all over again.

"I don't mean in general. I have a great job, wonderful friends and a family who loves me but... yeah... I suck at this."

"At sex?"

"No, I don't suck at sex, although maybe I do. It's been a really long time." Then she covered her face. "I shouldn't be telling you all this. You're a complete stranger." She looked at him from between her fingers.

"Talking helps." He shrugged.

Ana took her hands away from her face.

He continued, "I'm a totally unbiased person who you'll probably never see again. Why haven't you had sex in a long time? You're an attractive female."

"It's because of the panic attacks. It's hard to meet someone when you have them at the drop of a hat. Dating? Forget about it. I had hoped that a one-night stand might cure me of this… anxiety."

"What do you do for a living?"

"I'm a nurse." She beamed. "I really love my job."

Winston could tell. "So, I take it you don't have these attacks at work?"

She shook her head. "No, I've never had one at the hospital. It's like I go into work-mode. I feel safe at work, and don't get them there. Things were going so well tonight. I had an attack a few weeks ago and prior to that it was months." She frowned. "I only seem to get them when I try to date. The one I had a couple of months ago was when my friend set me up on a blind date. I was so sure I was over them. It was awful. We had barely said hello and my heart started to race. The worst part is that there's nothing I can do about it. There is no logic to it. I'm an intelligent person, yet…" She chewed on her lower lip, looking more and more agitated.

"What happened a few weeks ago?"

She pulled a face and sighed. "I decided to try internet dating. Such a stupid idea."

Winston smiled. "It's not stupid."

"I ended up puking on the guy before we could place our appetizer order."

"Oh! I'm sure he understood… after you explained things."

She shook her head, looking down at her lap. "I fainted; he left before I could come to."

"Bastard mother fu—" He grit his teeth for a few seconds. There were tons of dickheads out there. "Good riddance. He is a loser and not worth your time."

She smiled, it was small and shy.

Winston breathed out through his nose. "What happened tonight then?"

"I don't know. I was doing so well. I went to the Dark Horse, had a couple of drinks. My friend and I checked you guys out." Her cheeks flushed. "Sorry!"

"No need to apologize." He shrugged. "It is what it is."

"Cody came up to me and we got to talking. I really enjoyed his company and I found him attractive. We ended up staying until the bar was closing. In hindsight, I may have dragged things out by asking for another drink and then another. I sipped really slowly. I should have recognized the signs. It's just that I was so happy. For once I had met a guy, a cute guy, I could talk to him without having an attack. I was so sure I would be able to see the night through and then…"

"You panicked."

"Yes, I panicked. When push came to shove, I lost it." She groaned, covering her face with her hands. "I'm such a loser." The words were muffled.

"You're not a loser. It sounds like you're making progress. Have you seen someone about this?"

She pulled her hands away and made eye contact. "I'm down to one session a week. I was doing so well."

"You *are* doing really well. You're talking to me."

"Yes, but it's not like… we're dating or about to hook up or anything." She narrowed her eyes. "What about you?" she asked. "What's going on with you? Why aren't you holed up for the night like all the rest of the shifters in town?"

"Nothing much to tell." He smiled.

Ana cocked her head. "Yeah right. A shifter not looking for a booty call on Shifter Night? There must be a story there."

"I guess I'm sick of all the hook-ups. I come into town once a month and screw some nameless female. We've been frequenting either the Dark Horse in Sweetwater or The Cock Inn in Smitherson for years. You do the math. I'm sick of it. I tried having a causal relationship – and I use the term loosely – but that doesn't work either. It seems that all the human females I've tried it with began to assume that we were together in a real relationship. This despite my only being in town one night a month. Nah! I'm done with all the meaningless sex. I want a real relationship."

"Two things, firstly, what I wouldn't do for sex, meaningless or otherwise." Then she blushed. "For the record, I've never had a one-night stand before." She pulled in a breath, looking mortified at her admission. "Secondly, why not just have a real relationship if you truly want one? I've heard – might just be rumors – that shifters and humans are in committed relationships. One of my friend, Eileen's, work colleagues disappeared to go and live in some settlement in the middle of nowhere, apparently."

"You're right, only I'm not on the list."

She frowned. "List? Cody was also talking about a list as well. What list?"

"Shifter females are practically non-existent. They just stopped being born. We ended up with a ninety-five to five, male/female ratio."

Ana gasped. "I didn't realize it was so bad."

"We were forced to look elsewhere for mates, hence looking to human females. Shifters and humans are highly compatible. Thing is, we can't just descend on the rural towns in the area and mate half the females. It might cause problems. So, for now, we all wait our turn to find a mate. A few males at a time. Bide our time. We live longer than humans so it's doable."

"Oh, I see." Her eyes widened. "The only time you really get to mingle with women is on Shifter Night."

"Exactly. We take turns coming into town to spend time with females. It's the only interaction most of us get."

"Oh no!" She chewed on her bottom lip. "Poor Cody."

"Forget about Cody. He's a fully grown male, quite capable of taking care of himself. You guys had a fun night, didn't you?"

"Yeah, but I'm sure he wanted sex and it'll be too late for him to pick up another woman."

"What do you take us for? We're not that desperate."

She widened her eyes.

Winston choked out a laugh. "Okay, maybe we are… not all of us though. Don't worry about Cody. He'll be just fine."

Ana smiled. It was wide and bright. It eased something in him to see her happy. Such a sweet, kind female deserved to be happy. "So, you're going to wait then? No more messing around until you make the list?"

Winston nodded. "Yep, I hope it doesn't take years, I doubt it will. A couple more months, a year max and I should reach the top."

"It'll be your turn?"

He nodded. "Yup, it'll be my turn. No more screwing around. I'm done with that. Done with being seen as a piece of meat and viewing females in the same way. It isn't right."

"Good for you. I really do hope you make that list soon." Ana stood up and smiled shyly at him. "I'd better get going." She gestured towards the parking area.

"Tell you what, why don't you come to the Dark Horse in a month. Come and have a drink with me."

Her eyes clouded. "No, you saw what happened. I

couldn't..."

"Relax, we can go as friends. I think it would do you good. That way you could put yourself out there a bit, talk with the males but with no need to worry. I'll have your back."

"I'm not sure —"

"You should get out, and you never know, maybe you will meet someone who blows you away. Someone you feel comfortable with."

Ana's chest rose and fell in quick succession. Was it happening again? Had he pushed too hard?

"Look," he put up a hand, "no pressure, okay? I'll be there in a month." *What am I saying?* He hadn't planned on going back to the Dark Horse. The place was a meat market. It was too late to take it back. "Come if you want. Bring your friend. Join me for a drink." He shrugged.

"I need to go." She pointed to the parking lot.

"I'll walk you. Or, I could give you a ride home."

She shook her head so hard her hair went flying. "That's okay. I'll manage."

"You sure? I wouldn't mind giving you a ride."

"Nah. Thanks for the offer but I'll be fine. I'm used to standing on my own two feet." She started to walk away. Her heels clacking softly on the pavement.

"Ana..."

She stiffened and then glanced back over her shoulder, "Yes?"

"For what it's worth, I don't think you're an idiot or a loser. I think that the right male would be understanding and patient."

She smiled. "Thanks." Then she was gone. Once she was far enough away, Winston followed, just to make sure she got her cab safely.

CHAPTER 7

Doctor Brenner put the end of her pen in her mouth for a second or two before pulling it back out. "I like the sound of this guy. He seems nice, genuine… and he sounds like he's seriously hot too." She lifted her brows and smiled. "I've heard a thing or two about the shifters… about Shifter Night." She got this strange look on her face. "Maybe I should hit the bar myself, I'm not getting any younger."

"They don't go to the Dark Horse to find love, they go for…" Ana felt her cheeks heat, "sex," she said it in a lowered tone.

"I know exactly why they come into town. Let me tell you, you think you're struggling… well so am I. I've been on several dates this year. I ended up having sex with two of the guys, even saw the one guy for a few months. I didn't have a single orgasm. I can't remember the last time I had one. I'm reaching a point where I'm ready to throw in the towel. I'm thirty-seven, unmarried and considering getting a cat."

"You should come with us then."

"Oh," her eyes glinted, "so you're going to go then?"

Ana frowned. "I don't know. I want to, I'm worried. Maybe." She sighed, wishing she had more guts.

"This Winston guy sounds sweet, he's not looking for love or sex, he sounds like a perfect candidate for role-playing. For helping you get over your phobia and working your way up some of the steps in the fear hierarchy. This method is tried and tested. It's called systematic desensitization, or graduated exposure therapy." Ana could see her therapist thinking as her eyes lifted to the ceiling before coming back to her. "You would start with a drink at the bar and progress to dinner and then maybe... hand-holding... then —"

"Hold up." She widened her eyes. "I don't even know this guy – Winston – he's offered to meet me for a drink, that's it." She shook her head. "He's not interested in dating me."

"Maybe he is. He sounds like he wants to help you. You should go for that drink, and if the two of you get along..." Doctor Brenner held up her hands, "as friends of course, you should ask him out on a friendly date. Ask him if he'll help you."

"I think you're jumping the gun just a bit." Ana clasped her hands together in her lap.

"You have nothing to lose though." Her therapist leaned forward in her chair. "I think you should go... my original prescription still stands," she paused. "You need to have fun."

Ana had enjoyed the short time she and Winston had spent together. It was one drink. What could it hurt? Sure, she might end up looking like a fool if she had an attack in the middle of the packed bar but maybe it would be worth it in the end.

CHAPTER 8

THREE WEEKS LATER...

"It was the best sex of my life," Edith gushed.

Ana fought not to roll her eyes. She'd already heard every minute detail of that night and several times.

"You really should give it another go." Her friend's voice was animated.

"No way!" Ana shook her head. "I'll go with you to the bar but only to get a drink. I'm not letting some guy pick me up."

"You're hoping to see him, aren't you?" Edith grinned.

"If he's there, he's there, if not then, whatever." Ana didn't really mean it, she *was* hoping to see the shifter with the beautiful light brown eyes and the gorgeous smile. Winston was sweet. She enjoyed talking to him. This way, at least if Edith ended up hooking up with one of them again, she wouldn't have to just stand around, or worse, feel another panic attack coming on and leave.

She refused to ruin Edith's evening by making her leave along with her. It had happened too many times to count, especially in the early days. She could do this. She *would* do this.

The cab pulled up to the sidewalk and they got out, thanking the driver. Edith hooked her arm with Ana's and they made their way into the bar. "How do you even walk on those things?" Ana looked down at her friend's heels.

Edith shrugged. "You do what you gotta do, right?"

"If you say so." Ana had taken it easy this time around. No hair products, no hectic make-up. She wore a pair of jeans, a cute halter-top with an open back and low heels. In other words, she was completely underdressed because the ladies who hit this bar on Shifter Night went all out. Ana wasn't there to find love or a hook-up or any of that though, she was here to have fun, that was it. She sucked in a deep breath, feeling her nerves settle.

They made their way through the throngs of people and found a gap at the bar. Okay, it was a tiny fissure in the wall of people. "I'm on it. Wait here," Edith yelled into her ear before wedging herself in. It seemed even busier than the last time. Minutes later and her friend was no closer to being served. This despite there being several people behind the bar area, all working their asses off.

Ana took a look around her, the ratio of women to men was also way off. There were at least five women to every man. The ladies were all ages and all shapes and sizes, clearly out on the prowl. They were out for blood. Shifter blood. It was a circus. She had to smile. She felt sorry for Winston if he was in amongst all this. The women weren't shy, they were going after what they wanted. Those days of guys hitting on and chasing the women were long gone. The tables had turned. She allowed her eyes to sweep the crowd.

So far though, no sign of him. Not that she was really looking. Ana wasn't desperate. Anyway, Winston was probably just being nice when he made the offer. He had most likely forgotten all about her. Edith had two hands on the bar now, so she was going to be served any time… maybe… surely… then again, none of the servers were even looking her way.

"You made it," his deep baritone seemed to fold itself around her.

Ana turned. She couldn't help but smile. "Hi! Yeah, I made it, but don't feel obliged to hang out or anything. I mean, you may have changed your mind about… you know… Shifter Night." She was babbling. She pursed her lips together to stop herself.

Winston smiled. He really was very good-looking. He wore a red checked shirt, something along the lines of what a lumberjack would wear. The material pulled tight over his broad shoulders. His thighs were encased in faded blue jeans that fit him just so. "Nah, I haven't changed my mind." He had to speak up so that she could her him above all the noise. Winston leaned in. He smelled really good. Ana felt sorry for all the women here with their eyes on him. She was sure there were quite a few. "Would you like something to drink?"

"I'm here with my friend, Edith." She pointed in the general direction. Edith had already been swallowed up by several rows of people, all looking to buy a drink. "She's in there, somewhere." Ana peered around a group of people waiting at the bar and spotted Edith, still waiting herself. "She's not having much luck though."

Winston nodded. "It can get crazy here on a Saturday." She needed to partly read his lips to know what he was saying.

"That's for sure!" she shouted.

"What are you guys drinking?" he cupped his hands around his mouth.

"A beer or a cider, something out of a bottle. I don't think glasses are going to work." As she said it, yet another person bumped into her. A young woman, also barely balancing on really high heels. She looked like she might have had too much to drink.

"Let me handle it." Winston turned and called to a guy close to the bar. A female bartender seemed to already be waiting to take his order. Go figure, she was only too eager to serve the gorgeous shifter. Although Ana couldn't hear a thing Winston said, the big shifter at the bar nodded. He turned and placed an order. Then Winston parted the people at the bar and returned with Edith who was grinning wildly. They went through the motions of introducing themselves to each other. Edith gave her an exaggerated wink, which she hoped Winston didn't see. Then she gave a double thumbs up to Ana when Winston turned his back. Ana felt her cheeks heat. She shook her head and mouthed 'no' but Edith just grinned at her. It was cheeky. Didn't her friend understand that it wasn't like that?

A woman approached Winston. She leaned up and said something in his ear. She was really pretty with long black hair and wide blue eyes.

Winston shook his head. The woman gripped his bicep and leaned in, talking a whole lot more. He listened and then shook his head again, saying something back.

The pretty lady shrugged and walked away.

Edith gripped her arm. "He wants you," she said, directly into Ana's ear.

"Stop!" Ana spoke under her breath but tried to sound forceful.

"It's true though." Edith winked at her. Her friend meant well, but she didn't always listen. "The guy likes you. You may as well admit it."

"It's not like that."

"It totally is and you should go for it." Edith smiled.

"I'm going to go if you don't stop. He's just a friend and that's it."

Edith put her arm around Ana. "I'm sorry. I didn't mean…"

Ana felt bad instantly. "It's okay. I know."

"It's just…" Her friend hugged her. "I want the best for you. I want you to be happy again."

"I *am* happy. I have a great job and awesome friends." She hugged Edith. "I have a family who loves me. I'm happy." She said it with conviction she didn't completely feel. Although she was happy in most aspects of her life, she still felt that something was missing.

"Not like you were. Not like when…"

Ana squeezed Edith's hand. "I'll be okay. I'm here, aren't I? I'm getting better. It's taking way longer than I would have hoped, but I'll get there." There was a nagging voice inside her that told her she was never going to get better. Not before she was old and gray at any rate. Ana ignored it.

"Yeah, you will. You know I'm always here for you, right?"

"I know." They hugged again.

The guy from the bar came up, holding several drinks

in is big hands. He handed Winston the drinks and winked at both her and Edith.

"I'm Zack." He shook Edith's hand and then took hers. "I'm very pleased to meet you."

Ana nodded, the guy didn't let go of her hand. He lifted it to his mouth and kissed her palm. It was way too intimate. "Can I get you a drink?" he asked, his eyes on hers.

"Um… you already did." Ana tried to take her hand back but the shifter held on tight.

Her heart started to beat a little quicker. There was a deep growl and the shifter let go of her in an instant. Zack held up both hands, he said something to Winston who was frowning deeply. The situation felt tense. Winston bristled, his shoulders seemed to broaden. If he put any more pressure on that shirt it was going to rip. His jaw was tight, then finally he nodded and the tension dissipated in an instant. Zack gave Winston a tap on the side of the arm. He nodded in what looked like understanding.

"Have a good evening, ladies!" he shouted, then he winked and disappeared into the throng.

Winston handed each of them their drinks. He leaned into Ana. "Sorry about that. Are you okay?" His eyes were filled with concern.

Ana leaned in. "I'm fine. Thanks for the save."

"Any time." His voice was really deep. Winston had what looked like a beer in his hand. He used it to point towards the back of the bar. She looked over to where he was pointing. It was a bit quieter on that end, away from the gyrating bodies on the dance floor and the hustle and bustle of the bar area itself.

Edith gripped her arm. "There's Jacob," her voice was

filled with excitement. Her eyes were wide. Jacob was Edith's hook-up from last time. She gave a squeal. "I forgot how sexy he is."

"Do you want to go over and say hi?"

Edith shook her head. "No, that's fine, I'll hang with you guys." She looked from Ana to Winston.

"Really!" Ana raised her brows. "It's okay," she spoke directly into Edith's ear, keeping her voice down. "He's really sweet, I'm sure I'll be okay." Ana knew that Edith was dying to go over to Jacob. She was just trying to be a good friend to Ana.

"You sure?" When Edith pulled back, she was frowning.

"Of course, just let me know if you leave or anything."

Edith smiled. She nodded, her eyes bright with excitement. "Same goes for you."

Ana rolled her eyes. "That's not going—"

"Only joking." Edith squeezed her arm and bounded off to Jacob who was just as her friend had described him. Tall, dark hair, tanned skin. Who was she kidding? They were all gorgeous. Every last one of them.

She turned back towards Winston, who was fending off another woman. This one had shoulder-length brown hair. She looked a little older. Winston grinned when they locked eyes. He became serious though as he turned his attention back to the woman, giving another shake of the head. This one was a bit more persistent. She even gripped him by the bicep and stood really close. Some people didn't respect personal space. She kept talking, moving closer and closer. Her mouth only millimeters away from Winston's ear. Her hand now stroked his arm. Winston looked tense. He didn't seem to be enjoying the attention. He shook his head.

Ana sighed. He'd rescued her so she felt it was only right to return the favor. "Hey, babe!" She put her arm around his waist, breaking the contact the other woman had. *Wow, he sure was big.* Winston towered over her. The music and general bar noise wasn't as bad over here, so the lady must have heard Ana.

"Hey…" He sounded shocked, but quickly pulled himself together. "Sweetheart," he added. Winston gave her a kiss on the top of her head. He put a hand on her back. The middle of her back, barely touching her. *Such a sweetie.*

Ana was thrilled to find that she wasn't affected. Her heart rate stayed normal. Her breathing as well. That feeling of her throat closing and the room becoming smaller didn't happen. They were just pretending after all, so it stood to reason that she wouldn't be affected. It felt good to have contact with another human being. Someone she didn't know. A guy. A really cute guy. Not that she was interested or anything.

The lady muttered something that sounded far too much like 'lucky bitch' and walked off.

Ana had to laugh. Winston released her. He laughed too. "Thanks."

"You saved me earlier so I thought I'd return the favor."

He narrowed his eyes into hers. "I told you I would take care of you. Seems we can help each other." He held out his beer. "To making new friends and having good clean fun!"

"To friends." She touched bottle necks with him and they both drank.

"So, how have you been?" he asked, taking another drink of his beer.

"Good." She shrugged. "Same old, really."

"All good on that… other front? Are you doing okay right now?" He looked at her intently.

She looked away before looking back at him. "I'm fine."

"You'll tell me if that changes right?"

"I don't want you to treat me like there's something wrong with me. I just want to have a good evening."

He sighed and ran a hand through his hair. "Sorry! I felt the need to check. Also, despite relaxing and having fun, you came here because I asked you to, so I feel a bit responsible."

"Well don't! I've been dealing with this for years." She paused. "I haven't gone out on any blind dates or frequented any establishments such as this so, no, no new panic attacks. My therapist agrees with you, by the way. She says I'm making progress."

"See. What did I tell you?"

"At this rate, I'll be forty-three by the time I can actually go on a real date with someone and forty-eight by the time I get to have sex again. Nineteen years is not so long to wait."

Winston shook his head. "I doubt it. You're being too hard on yourself. How was work?" She noticed how he changed the subject.

"Great! It's been a weird week though." She took a sip of her drink.

"How so?" Winston frowned, waiting for her to continue. He looked sincerely interested so she continued.

"We have this patient. He's your average run-of-the-mill middle-aged guy who recently caught his wife cheating. He ran after the man who was in bed with her.

Chased him into the backyard and over the gate – which was locked, so they had to climb over it. The gate was pretty high, so when he landed on the other side, he broke both his legs."

"No!"

"Yes!" she said.

"Talk about bad luck." Winston was smiling.

"I know, poor guy. His wife served him divorce papers yesterday. Her husband is in the hospital with badly broken legs and she serves him. Some people are cruel."

Winston clenched his jaw. "I don't understand you humans sometimes." He shook his head. "We shifters mate for life. We would never even think to cheat. Once we fixate on a person, we stop noticing anyone else in that way."

"Hey, don't put us all in the same category." His way of thinking irritated her. "I would never —"

"Damn… sorry! I didn't mean you. I swear! It's just, it happens a lot. That lady you saved me from just now…" He raised his brows.

"Yeah?" she said when he didn't elaborate.

"Well, I could scent that she is mated, yet she is here trying to hook up with one of us. It's so wrong. I was about to tell her where to get off when you came and saved my ass."

"Oh, I see," she huffed out a breath. "That's bad. Some people are terrible. So shifters don't cheat?"

He shook his head. "Nope."

"Not ever?"

"It's not in our DNA. Once we are with someone, it's for life."

"So that's it for you then? Until you meet Miss Right,

that is? Only one more woman for you… ever."

Winston gave a shy smile. "Yup, that's the plan."

"I think it's commendable."

He looked over her shoulder. Ana turned just as Edith came up to them. "I'm going to the bar with some of the guys!" she yelled. "We're getting more shots. Do you want a couple?" She raised her brows, looking from Ana to Winston and back again.

Ana shook her head. "We're good… unless?" She glanced at Winston, who shook his head.

"Nope, we're good."

"Okay. See you later," Edith yelled as she turned and started walking towards the bar.

"Okay!" Ana yelled after her. She watched her friend join a group of people already headed for the bar. They were a mix of both men and women.

She glanced over at Winston. He was such an attractive guy. Could be standing with any of the women in there. "So, why did you come tonight? Don't tell me it was only to keep my sorry ass company?"

His forehead creased. "You should stop putting yourself down like that, Ana. I happened to enjoy your company the other night. I had hoped to see you again." He paused, taking a sip of his beer. "I also like coming to Sweetwater. I enjoy unwinding and having a few beers." He held up the bottle in his hand. "Just because I don't want to fall into bed with the first pretty female I see doesn't mean I don't want to spend time with one and quite frankly, most females in Sweetwater just want one thing from us shifters and it isn't conversation. I guess I know I'm safe with you." He grinned.

Ana had to laugh. "Okay then." She felt her cheeks heat. "You are definitely safe with me." She gave another chuckle. "I apologize. I do keep putting myself down, you're right, it's something I should stop. It's just, I've had this problem for a long time now, just over four years and it's just so hard…" She scrunched up her nose. "There I go again with the complaining."

Winston touched the side of her arm. "You're still being hard on yourself."

"I wish I could control it but I can't. When that feeling starts up, it takes over. Just when I think I might have a handle, it hits me upside the head."

"Do you know the cause? You say the episodes started four years ago. That's pretty specific on the timing. There must be a reason why you get these attacks? You didn't always have this problem."

CHAPTER 9

For a few seconds, it seemed like she was going to shut down but then she sucked in a deep breath and licked her lips. She looked him in the eyes and began to speak. "Um… it all started out fine. An evening out. I didn't even want to go. I can't tell you how many times I wished we hadn't..." She looked somewhere over his shoulder. "We were walking to the car after a dinner-date. It was a half a block on a well-lit street. It wasn't all that late yet and it's not like Sweetwater is a dangerous place to live. It's a low crime area. It had only just turned nine. One minute we were walking and the next we had a gun in our faces. The guy was alone. He wore a ski-mask. I could see the fear in his eyes. His hands were shaking. He demanded we hand over our possessions. My rings, our watches, wallets. Instead of complying John retaliated." He could see her disappear into her own mind. Her eyes clouded in thought and those thoughts didn't appear to be pleasant.

"The guy insisted. The shaking got worse. I screamed at John to do as he said but he shook his head and told the guy to piss off. Next thing the weapon went off, his face exploded in a spray of blood." She wiped away a tear. Her whole face had a look of horror. "I still hear the sound of the shot, still see the mangled mess that was left of John's head." She wiped away a couple more tears. "Our attacker went nuts. He kept on saying 'Oh god! Oh god!' Over and over. He dropped the gun and made a run for it. Turned out he was a petty thief who had done time before, his prints were on the gun. The guy, James Simons, said that it was an accident. He didn't mean to shoot. He accidentally squeezed the trigger and..." She shrugged. "It being an accident won't bring John back though." She dug around in her bag and pulled out a wad of tissues.

Fuck! No wonder she suffered from panic attacks. He didn't want to push. Winston kept quiet, waiting to see what else she was willing to divulge.

Ana blew her nose softly. "It affected me. For months I couldn't even leave my house. It was two years of random panic attacks. I'd get them if someone jogged past me or if someone walked up to me unannounced. I'd get them at home, if someone knocked on my door. The nightmares were almost worse. I couldn't sleep. I still struggle with them. I guess I might battle with trust. I don't know. Realistically, the chances of being attacked again in this way are small to none, especially here in Sweetwater. At least the really bad days are over. I couldn't work for over a year."

"You are a strong female."

She shook her head. "Why can't I get on with my life then? Why does the prospect of dating someone affect me so badly?"

"You went through a terrible ordeal. It's to be

expected. It's also not your fault. You're stronger than you think."

"You're sweet to say so."

Winston had to ask. "Who was the male you were with, the one who was killed that night? I think you said his name was John."

She shrugged, trying to look nonchalant. It didn't work, he noticed the tension in her shoulders, the tightness of her jaw. "Someone I was… with at the time." He got the feeling the male had meant something to her but again, he didn't want to push.

"So you associate dating with being attacked."

She looked down at her clasped hands. "I guess. I don't think it's as simple as that though, or I would have figured this out by now."

Winston couldn't help but feel that there was something she wasn't telling him. She pulled at a cuticle on one of her nails. Winston gripped her hand, using his other hand, he tilted her chin up so that she faced him. "You are brave. You went through a terrible ordeal. One most people never have to go through. You have made enormous progress. You said you couldn't work and didn't want to leave your home in the beginning and now, here you are."

She gave a shy smile. "I guess you're right. Sometimes you move forwards so slowly that it doesn't even feel like you've moved at all. You have to glance back to notice the change."

"Exactly right." He paused. "You mentioned your therapist a few times, so you are still working on it?"

Ana nodded. "Doctor Brenner encouraged me to come tonight despite how things turned out the last time… not that I'm here for the same reason," she quickly added.

"You mentioned *me* to your therapist?" He smiled.

Her cheeks turned distinctly red and she looked away.

"No need to be embarrassed about it," he quickly added, not liking that she felt uncomfortable about it.

She nodded. "I did tell her about our meeting. She insisted I start having some fun."

"I think I like this female." He grinned.

"She told me to come tonight, said I needed to work on desensitizing myself around the whole dating thing."

He felt himself frown. "Desensitizing yourself?"

"It's nothing." She waved a hand. "She wants me to role-play, to fake date." Ana laughed, sounding embarrassed. "It's apparently an honest to god therapy where you slowly expose yourself to higher levels of the thing you're most afraid of but I'm not so sure about it. I don't even know how it would work." She widened her eyes.

"Interesting." He reached out and clasped her hand, almost expecting her to flinch. Although Ana didn't take his hand back, she also didn't pull away. "Thank you for trusting me with your story, but I think it's time to have a bit of fun – like your doctor ordered. Do you want to dance?" An upbeat tune blared from the jukebox.

Ana pursed her lips for a second and then she gave a nod. "Why not?" She rolled her eyes. "Doctor Brenner would insist if she was here."

Winston squeezed her hand and led her to the dance floor. They danced their asses off for the next forty-five minutes. Ana could shake those hips. Her cheeks became flushed and her eyes sparkled. She squealed every time a new song came on, declaring that it was her favorite. It was great seeing her let loose a little. Ana was as sexy as hell. He could see that she wasn't wearing a bra, her breasts weren't very big so she could get away with it. Winston tried not to stare but fuck, she was a stunner. Not that he was interested in her in that way, but he'd have to be deaf, dumb and blind not to notice that her nipples were very much out there and how her breasts bounced as she danced. Small bounces but fucking bounces none-the-less. He was a prick but he couldn't help it.

A slow song came on. The beat heavy, yet measured and rhythmical. Ana looked up at him from under her lashes, she gave the tiniest of half-smiles. He could see a look of regret register on her face for a moment. Then she turned to leave the dance floor.

"Hey." Winston grabbed her hand and turned her back. "Are you going to leave me hanging?" She was incredibly sweet and sensitive. It seemed so unfair that she was plagued with these attacks. That a moment in her life had brought about such devastating consequences.

Ana narrowed her eyes. "I'm not sure if…"

Winston kept ahold of her hand. "If you start to feel uncomfortable, in any way, tell me and we can stop." He squeezed her hand. "No pressure! None whatsoever. We're friends remember? Also, your doctor said that a bit of role-playing would help you, so what do you say we give it a try?"

She sucked in a deep breath and gave a nod. "Yeah, okay. That would be nice. I haven't done this since…" She stopped herself. "In a very long time," she mumbled.

"Come here." Winston pulled her closer to him. "You tell me if you need to stop. I promise I won't mind."

Ana reached up and put her arms around his neck. He

gripped her hips. It seemed like the safest place to put his hands. That way, there would be distance between them. He smiled at her. "See, not so bad."

She smiled back. Her stunning blue eyes sparkled. The disco ball turned above them. "No, not at all."

They swayed to the music. She scented of something lightly floral. Her hair of coconut. She was soft and warm. Winston almost felt disappointed when a rock song started not too long after and he was forced to release her.

"Thank you!" She smiled up at him. "That was... nice."

"Do you want—?"

Ana's friend walked up to them, she was frowning. She leaned in, speaking under her breath to Ana. "Jacob is flirting with one of the other women. Do you think he plans on taking her back to the hotel? I kind of just thought we would... you know. That we would..." She left the sentence hanging. "Not that I'm looking for a relationship or anything."

"Why not hang with us then?" Ana said, also under her breath. "Don't go back if he seems to be into someone else."

Edith seemed to think on it for a moment. "Nah! We had such a good time, I'm sure he's not trying to blow me off."

Ana nodded. "You know where we are. Let me know if you decide to leave with him."

"I will. Are you having fun?" Edith smiled.

"I am, actually." Ana smiled back.

Edith nodded. "I'm glad." Her friend winked at her. "See you later."

"Yeah."

Edith headed back towards the bar, making her way around groups of people. It wasn't quite as busy as before.

"So…" Ana stuck her hands in her pockets.

"So…" He did the same. "I'm glad you're having fun."

"You heard that?" She lifted her brows.

"Yes, I did." He frowned. "I told you that the males are reluctant to spend more than one night with the same female on account of them becoming attached. I think your friend might already like Jacob a little too much."

"I think you're right, she hasn't stopped talking about him." She looked worried, lines creased her brow. "She'll probably be hurt if he ends up leaving with that other woman."

Winston sighed. "It's probably better if he doesn't take her back with him. I know that sounds terrible, but if she's already developing feelings for him it'll only get worse if they spend another night together."

"Yeah, regardless of what happens, I don't think we should be hanging around the Dark Horse on Saturdays anymore. It's obviously not good for Edith. I told her that she'd be useless at one-night stands. Looks like I was right, she's far too emotional."

He fought back disappointment at the prospect of not seeing her again. "I am glad you came this evening. You are definitely making progress. I like to think I had a hand in that."

She pulled a face, like he was a crazy person. "I can hang out at a bar with someone. You're a friend, so I feel fine hanging out. It would be different if the guy was an actual prospect, like a real date. Or if I actually wanted to…" She widened her eyes. "You know… have sex." She was so cute the way she said it. At the same time, he was a little put out that she didn't see him in that way. Then again, it was part of the reason he enjoyed her company. No strings attached and all that. This female didn't see him like just a piece of meat. It was refreshing.

"Come back next month," he blurted.

She looked at him skeptically.

"No, really! We can pretend date. Do that role-play thing your doctor said would help you." *What the fuck?* He'd never dated before, now he was asking a human to fake date him? He needed his brain checked.

Ana narrowed her eyes.

Her aversion to the idea made him want to take her out even more. "Here." He took out his cellphone. "What's your number?"

"Why?" She folded her arms across her chest. "Why do you want to fake date me?"

"I told you, I want to help you. I haven't been approached by any more females looking for a hook-up. It's because we're... together and I'm having a good time. Let's help each other. I'll call when I'm back in town next month. I'll take you on a date. We can dress up and go out somewhere nice. I'll open the door for you and hold your hand... the whole nine yards. I'm hoping you don't have one of your attacks but if you do, I'll help you through it. It'll be fun to spend time with a female... *with you...* without... any expectations."

Ana looked thoughtful. "Like I said, Doctor Brenner did mention that role-play might help to desensitize me. I would have tried it with a friend of mine but he isn't half as gorgeous." She widened her eyes, looking shocked at the admission. "I didn't mean it like that." Then she looked totally appalled. "Not at all. It's just that I don't think it would work with Tom because I know him too well, I see him as more of a brother."

Winston grinned. She may not see him in that way but she did find him attractive. "It's fine. It's not like that between us, right?" He raised his brows.

She snorted. "No, of course not." He noticed her gaze move towards the bar. He also looked in that direction. It was Edith, the female did not look happy. She was arguing with Jacob. "It doesn't look like it's going to work out between them."

"Not such a bad thing considering he can't have a relationship. Here…" He handed her his phone. "Give me your number. Next time it'll be just the two of us. I'll even pick you up."

"I still don't get why you want to help me."

"I like you. I enjoy your company. I would love to fake date the hell out of you. I told you, we don't have many females where I come from. I don't want to have meaningless sex anymore but I still enjoy the company of the fairer sex. I know I'm safe with you." He winked at her. *What the hell?* He didn't wink at females, or beg them to hang out with him. There was something about this female. A deep-seated sadness. The pain in her eyes. He wanted to help her. Had enjoyed watching her smile and have fun. He enjoyed spending time with her and that was really the bottom line.

She laughed. "Yeah, okay. Are you sure though? Have you ever seen anyone in the throes of a panic attack? A real panic attack? I was still okay the other night. I wasn't too bad yet. I don't want —"

"I'm sure. Shifters don't scare easily." He thrust his phone in her hand just as Edith arrived.

Her eyes were blazing. Her face flushed. "He left with the other girl." Ana's friend looked like she was about to burst into tears. Her lip even quivered.

"Oh, honey." Ana threw her arms around Edith and they hugged for a few seconds. Edith sniffed and wiped her eyes as they pulled away. Yup, she was crying.

Winston didn't know what to do, where to look or how to respond. Jacob had done the right thing, only, he suspected that Edith did not want to hear that right now.

Ana put her arm around Edith. "Let's get a drink. He's an asshole for—"

Edith shook her head. "I would prefer it if we left. I want to go home and have a hot shower. There's a tub of ice-cream in the freezer with my name on it. It's double chocolate."

"Double chocolate will work every time. Okay," Ana nodded, "let's go then."

"Why don't you stay?" Edith glanced his way. "I can catch a cab if—"

"Rubbish!" Ana gripped her friend by the upper arm. "We came together and we'll leave together. How many times have you left early because of me?"

"But you guys seem—"

"No but's. It's about time I returned the favor." Ana pushed a few buttons on his phone. Then she pushed a few more before handing it back to him.

"You're positive you want to do this next month?" She looked unconvinced. "You are welcome to change your mind and I won't mind in the least.

"Are you kidding? I'm definitely sure. Hey, can I give you guys a ride?"

Ana shook her head. "No, don't worry about it. We're good."

He hooked his thumbs in his jeans pockets. "You sure? I don't mind."

"I'm sure. Thanks for the fun evening. I enjoyed myself."

He wasn't surprised she had turned him down. This female was used to doing everything for herself. "Me too." It was true, he had. Without thinking, Winston wrapped his arms around her and hugged her in much the same way she had done with Edith. She sucked in air, clearly shocked, but she still returned the hug. The scent of coconut and flowers filled his nose.

Then he and Edith said their goodbyes and he watched as they made their way through the busy bar, finally leaving.

He really hoped she took him up on his offer. He was excited at the prospect of going on a fake date with her. Yup, he was definitely losing his mind.

CHAPTER 10

E dith dipped her spoon into the rich dark ice-cream and scooped a large helping into her mouth. She sucked on the treat for a few seconds before chewing a few times. She savored the dessert, leaning back on the sofa, eyes closed until she finally swallowed, eliciting a low moan. "It's almost better than orgasming, almost but not quite. Jacob was so much better than any ice-cream I ever had, chocolate or otherwise. I can't believe he left with that hussy instead of me." She gave her spoon another lick before dipping it back in the tub.

"He's not allowed to date – to have any kind of relationship. You need to try not to take it personally. Even if he did really like you, and I'm sure he did, he couldn't act on it."

Edith looked at Ana pointedly. "Winston asked you out on a date."

Ana gave a little snort. "That's different. It's fake dating... not the real thing."

"Fake dating?" Edith cocked her head. "Yeah right, tell me another one. You warned me that I was too emotional for a one-night stand well, right back at ya."

"It's not like I'm going to sleep with him. We're friends, that's all."

"Don't forget that I saw him." Edith laughed. "He's too hot to be a friend."

"What a terrible thing to say. That's awful and so stereotypical. Next you'll tell me that men and women, in general, can't just be friends."

"Of course they can but only if there's no sexual attraction. You can't tell me you haven't noticed how sexy Winston is, how broad his shoulders are, how thick his biceps were in that shirt he was wearing tonight or how he filled those jeans," she raised her brows and widened her eyes, "and yes, I'm talking about the crotch area."

Ana choked out a laugh and covered her mouth with her hand. "I can't believe you said that," she finally managed to get out.

"It's the truth isn't it? The guy is packing."

"Edith!" Ana chided. "You can't say things like that and no, I can't say I noticed his… his… you-know-what. That's just plain rude."

"Really?" Her friend looked shocked. "You seriously didn't notice? You didn't look? Not even once?"

Ana shook her head so hard that she might give herself whiplash if she wasn't careful. "No way! Just no."

"Okay then… you can fake date him in that case. I guess you do see him as just a friend." She lifted her eyes in thought for a few seconds. "I don't understand what's in it for him though. He might have ulterior motives." Edith held the tub out to her.

"I don't think so." Ana scooped some ice-cream onto her own spoon. "He told me he's done screwing around."

"Famous last words." Edith wrinkled her nose.

"I believe him. You should have seen how many gorgeous women approached him this evening. He said they just want sex from him but he wants to have a bit of fun without those kinds of expectations. Thing is," she sucked in a breath, "we kind of both want the same thing, and I think he genuinely wants to help me."

"What do you want out of it?"

Ana sucked in a breath and then slowly released it. "I think I agree with Doctor Brenner, I want to have a bit of fun." She shrugged. "No more and no less. Just a little fun and if it helps me… get better." She couldn't bring herself to say the other words hovering on the edge of her mind… 'move on.' Guilt flooded her for wanting that.

"In that case," Edith smiled, "go for it." She winked at Ana. "I know I would."

Ana couldn't get ahead of herself though. A month was a very long time. Everything could change between now and then. She needed to discuss this with her therapist. She needed to give it more thought.

Fun.

No strings.

Just friends.

Was it possible? She may not have noticed the size of his package. *Did women actually check that out on a guy? Did they really?* She may not have noticed that, but she *had* noticed that Winston was a good-looking guy. That didn't mean she would ever end up liking him for real. It wasn't like he would ever be in town enough for that to happen. Real relationships took a long time to develop and that happened when people were seeing each other all the time. Nope, she was good. Something that felt a little like excitement unfurled in her. The prospect of fake dating Winston was sounding more and more appealing by the second.

CHAPTER 11

ONE MONTH LATER...

A na looked at her reflection in the mirror. Her bed was covered in clothes. She pulled on the hem of her dress. It was too short. Maybe it was too much. It was the proverbial little black dress but on steroids, since the sleeves were black lace. She wore a pair of heels, which felt a bit on the high side. Especially considering she wasn't used to wearing this type of shoe. Her toes were already pinching a bit. She had to say though, she did look really good in them. They made her legs look longer and her calves firmer. The whole outfit made her look really good. *Too good maybe?*

Why did she care? It wasn't like this was a real date or anything. That was the thing, she shouldn't care. If she wore this she might look like she did, when she didn't. Her heart sped up and her hands felt clammy. She sank down onto the edge of the bed and put a hand to her chest. The feeling didn't escalate. Her mouth didn't feel dry. There was an odd feeling in her stomach and her heart was beating a bit too fast but other than that she was okay.

Shit! She realized with a start, she was excited about going out tonight. This wasn't the start of a panic attack, it was excitement for the night ahead. She blew out a slow, easy breath.

She smiled. This was good for her. Winston was right. Her therapist had also urged her to take him up on his offer, so when the text message had come through earlier that day, she'd agreed to let him pick her up and take her out. Her smile widened. A fake date was just what the doctor ordered. Quite literally.

Ana stood up and smoothed her dress. This was too much though. She thought about changing into a pair of slacks and a nice top.

Just then, her doorbell rang. She looked at her watch. If that was Winston, he was ten minutes early. Who else could it be though? No one. There was no one else who would be ringing her doorbell this time of the evening on a Saturday.

She made her way to the entrance hall and looked through the peephole. *Oh god!!* She leaned her forehead against the wood. Her view of the shifter had been distorted and yet she could still see how incredible he looked. He wore a dark blue button-up collared shirt. His hair looked trimmed. He had that whole five o'clock shadow thing going on. His eyes were a beautiful golden-brown. They reminded her of a wolf's eyes. A shiver ran up her spine.

Fake date. This is just a fake date. She was going to prove to Edith that a man and a woman could just be friends. She waited a little longer to make sure her throat didn't close, that the room didn't close in. Okay then. All seemed well. Maybe she should pack a brown paper bag just in case.

"Are you going to let me in?" There was amusement laced in every deeply spoken word.

"Yes, of course," she quickly blurted way too loudly. She undid both of the deadbolts, one after the other and removed the chain. Then she unlocked the door and opened it. Lastly, she unlocked the security gate. "You're early," she announced, putting her hands on her hips. "I'm not ready, yet."

He whistled low, pretending to give her the once-over. "You look ready to me."

"Well, I'm not. I need to change. I also need to touch up my makeup and—"

He gently gripped her elbow. "No, you don't need to do any of those things. You look stunning. Almost too good considering this is a fake date."

"Exactly," she blurted. "You are completely right." She felt mortified. Hopefully he wouldn't get the wrong idea. "I knew it! I've gone overboard…" She could feel her cheeks heat. What must he think of her? "I'll just—"

He gave her a sexy half-smile. "You are not changing. I'm glad you made the effort. Also, from here on out we are *not* going to think of this as a fake date." He ushered her into the room, closing the door behind him.

"We're not?" She could feel herself frown.

He shook his head. "No, we aren't. It *is* a fake date but we're going to pretend it's real. We're role-playing, remember?"

"You have a point. Okay, fine… no problem but I still think I should change."

"You have great legs, I plan on looking at them all evening and therefore I vote you stick with the dress.

Please." He put his hands together as if in prayer.

She choked out a laugh. "You are too much, you know that? Fine, but I'm changing out of these heels."

"I fucking love the heels. The heels stay." His nostrils flared, his gaze firmly on her choice of shoes, then they moved up to her legs, taking their sweet time. Then up and up… Winston eyeballed her body. As in… took a long, hard look.

Her cheeks heated some more. Much more. Her neck felt hot. Even her eyeballs felt hot. Her hair seemed to prickle. He looked even better than he had a moment ago. Broad shoulders, dark blue jeans, unruly hair. It looked like he'd tried to tame it though. His eyes sparkled as they finally locked with hers.

This had all started over her heels and the fact that they were too high. She cleared her throat. "I… um… I… might fall over."

"Not going to happen." He took hold of her hand. "I've got you. I'll even carry you if need be. Shifters are really strong."

"Oh really!"

"We're super-human."

She chuckled. "Really now, because I'm soooo heavy," she said in a mocking tone.

He narrowed his eyes and turned serious in an instant. "Not even close. You are a tiny human. Smaller than most." He totally thought she was serious. It was cute.

"I was only joking. Okay, fine." She rolled her eyes. "I'll stay dressed like this but I need to put some lipstick on."

He pulled a face. "No, you don't need that gunk."

"For your information, I like wearing lipstick."

He narrowed his eyes to show his distaste.

"Fine, some lip gloss then?"

"I don't like the taste of all that rubbish."

Taste.

Taste?

As in on his tongue?

Really?

Her mouth fell open and her eyes felt like they were about to fall out of her head, they were bugging out that far.

"Don't look so shocked. We're on a date – that means I get to hold your hand, put my arm around you and hopefully, maybe just maybe, I get to kiss you at some point."

Her heart went nuts in her chest. That queasy feeling was back as a whole kaleidoscope of butterflies took flight in her stomach. It was just nerves. She was afraid of this ending badly. As in, with her face stuffed in a paper bag in the corner of a restaurant. Or even worse, lights out on the floor in the manager's office with a rescue team on the way. She'd been there before and didn't want it happening again.

"It would just be a kiss." He squeezed her hand. "Or two. You would be okay with a kiss or two, wouldn't you? We can make them small kisses."

"Yes… if they were small ones… I guess so." She licked her lips. "But only if you think we need to go that far." She frowned. "I'm not sure we need to go that far."

"We're role-playing here. We should do a good job of it."

"You're right." She licked her lips again and he tracked the movement.

"In fact," his gaze was still glued to her mouth, "I think we should get that pesky first kiss out of the way right now."

"Now?" Her voice was a bit shrill and she was breathing too quickly, but more out of excitement than panic. At least, she hoped it wasn't panic. It was difficult to tell anymore.

He frowned. "Only if you feel you can handle…"

Oh she so could. Ana was done with being afraid. She had to try. Ana gripped his shirt and pulled him down to her level. She planted one on him. One quick touch of the lips… only… once her mouth touched his, something ignited in her. Something bright and fierce. Something a little out of control.

Ana moaned. All out freaking moaned. Contact with the opposite sex just felt that darned good. As she moaned, her mouth opened. Then their tongues were fighting. Literally at war with one another, yet in sync. It was weird, yet amazing. Hardcore, passionate and all-consuming.

The air seemed to thin. Ana struggled to breathe. It seemed he had the same problem because the sound of their ragged breathing filled the room.

Winston pulled away first. Thank god, because she didn't think she was capable. Not that she wanted more, it was just that it had been so long since she'd done this. Too long.

Her chest expanded and contracted in rapid succession. Her hands still clasped his shirt. Two tight fists. "Oops!" she said.

Winston chuckled. "So much for a small kiss. Wow!"

Ana finally found it within herself to let him go. "It's just that I haven't done that in the longest time. I'm sorry. Flip I—"

"No need to apologize. If you're apologizing, then I

should too."

"Why are you apologizing? It was me doing all the moaning and grabbing and—"

"It takes two to tango," Winston interjected. "Look, I'm a guy, I'm going to react to a beautiful female even if you are my friend. As long as we have an understanding, we'll be okay."

She nodded, the whole kiss replaying in her mind. "No more kissing then?" It had been too much. As much as it had felt right, it was wrong. So very wrong. They couldn't do that again.

"Oh there'll be lots more kissing. We're fake dating so," he shrugged, "goes without saying."

Oh flip! He wanted more. "Um... sure, but not like that. We need to keep it..." *Controlled. Fake. Boring.* "Small... small kisses. Friendly kisses."

His eyes darkened but he gave a nod. "Yes, you're right, and no sex."

Why did he even bring that up?

"No sex," he repeated, his voice a little deeper. He said it like he needed her to agree.

"Absolutely not," she blurted, shaking her head with too much vigor.

"What do you say we hit the town?"

"Sounds good." Ana wasn't sure how she felt. Off balance was probably a good description. She felt light-headed, happy but there was also an underlying nervousness. An unease. Maybe she was just worried about a panic attack still sneaking up on her. It would probably happen when she let her guard down. It couldn't happen.

"You okay?" Winston narrowed his eyes on hers. Even took a step closer to her.

She forced a smile. "I'm good."

"You tell me if that changes."

She nodded, her smile coming easier. "I will." They set out into the night. There were so many possibilities out there. So many of them weren't for her though. Not for her.

CHAPTER 12

ONE WEEK LATER...

Her step felt lighter. Her smile brighter, more real. Edith was coming to dinner tonight. Ana had also invited a colleague from work. The new lady? New wasn't correct though since Shanna had been working at Sweetwater Hospital for two months already. She wasn't new anymore. It just struck her the other day, Monday to be exact, that she hadn't made an effort to get to know any of the new people at work and as a result, there were a whole bunch of folks who she barely said two words to. It was wrong. She'd been making an effort since. How could she not? It was incredibly wrong that there were orderlies whose names she didn't even know. It was rude of her.

Ana had decided on lasagna, bread and salad for dinner. She turned down the aisle that housed the pasta and stopped in her tracks. A family. They were right there. A mom, a dad, an older daughter of about three or four… and…

She took a step back as her eyes landed on the baby in the stroller. The little one was small yet plump, with tiny hands and fingers, and big round eyes. The child gurgled and smiled as the dad made raspberries. The mom said something and all three of them laughed. The baby squealed with excitement, little legs kicking vigorously. So very cute that it took her breath away. This was the reason she'd pulled away from most people at work. They had families. They talked about their kids and their lives like it was no big deal when it *was* a big deal... it was to Ana. Most of them were oblivious to how lucky they had it.

Her hands tightened further on the handle, her eyes still drawn to the family, she was waiting for the pain to flood. It was weird though because her heart didn't clench, that fist of hurt didn't close around her torso or dig its way into her mind. It was supposed to go into overdrive thinking of all the possibilities. *If only...*

Normally, she would've turned the other way, left even. Abandoned her shopping cart right there and walked out. Cancelled her plans for the evening.

Instead of doing all that, she licked her lips, gripped the handle tighter and stepped forward. One step and then another. One breath at a time until she was right up close to them.

Still no flare of pain. No need to run away. She picked up a box of pasta sheets. Going through the motions like any normal person would.

Normal.

This is normal.

I'm normal.

The family continued to chatter and joke. The baby gurgled. The little girl laughed. Within a minute, they moved off. They moved away from her and not the other way around. It felt so good. It felt empowering. Ana put the pasta into the cart. She was grinning broadly, the smile faltered though because that other feeling was back.

"Okay so, let me get this straight." Doctor Brenner was frowning. "You went out on a date, you kissed the guy."

"He told me to." Ana felt her cheeks heat. "I would never have done it otherwise," she mumbled the last.

"Yeah, yeah… whatever. It's not important who kissed who, what's important is that it happened. You played tonsil hockey with him, something, up until recently, you could only have dreamed about doing. It's amazing! It's fantastic and yet, you're moping about it. Why do you think that is?"

Ana shrugged. "I don't know." She paused, mulling it over. "I don't understand it. One minute I was elated it had happened. All I wanted was to do it again." She remembered how her whole body had hummed. "And then, I felt it, this feeling of unease. It didn't feel right inside."

"You say you felt the feeling again after you handled seeing that family in the supermarket?" Her therapist raised her brows.

Ana, leaned back in her chair. She nodded. "Yup. Instead of the hurt, the pain, the feeling of loss, I felt fine… I felt okay and then that feeling came back."

"How would you label this feeling? You said unease, can you elaborate?" Her therapist kept her eyes on her.

Ana knew from experience that Doctor Brenner would wait as long as it took for her to answer. "No, not really…" she shrugged. "I just didn't feel right. It felt wrong to feel happy… that's all."

"Why do you think that is?"

Twenty questions. She didn't feel like answering. It all felt too much like going round in circles, only, she was making progress, Ana could hold onto that.

"Why do you think your feeling good – happy even – would make you feel unease… as you put it?"

"I don't know. Like so many other things, I don't understand it." Ana could hear the frustration in her voice.

"Do you think it might be guilt?"

"No!" she answered too quickly, too sharply. "No, I don't think it was guilt." On the inside though, her mind raced. *Shit! Was it guilt?* They'd talked about this before. Unease… guilt… it might have been. She used to feel guilty… very guilty, but she'd moved past that, hadn't she? Hadn't she?

"You still haven't given yourself permission to move on," Doctor Brenner went on, "You feel guilty again, after all this time because you have finally started the process."

"That's crazy." Again, she answered too quickly, her voice elevated. "Why would I still feel guilty… about starting the process?" She lifted her eyes in thought. "John would want me to… carry on with my life. I need to…" *Move on.* Shit, she still couldn't say it. Maybe she was struggling with it more than she realized. "Do it," she finally said.

"Survivor's guilt. You lived and he died. You can't move on… you won't."

Again with the survivor's guilt. "It can't be, doc. I have no reason to feel guilty for what happened that night. We've been through this. I've worked through this. I had nothing to do with the shooting. There was nothing I could have done differently. Nothing I could have said or done to prevent it from happening. I didn't even want to go out that night, John talked me into it."

"You're alive, Ana, it's as simple as that. You're alive and starting to finally live again and it's making you feel those feelings of guilt."

"What do I do though? How do I stop myself from feeling this way when I have nothing to feel guilty about?" She could hear the frustration in her voice. It was a question she had asked before. Doctor Brenner had never had an answer for her. Nothing substantial at least. Her doctor had always told her that time and patience would get her there. The frustrating thing was that although her feelings of hurt had subsided and her panic attacks had dried up, at least for now, her feelings of guilt had grown.

Doctor Brenner smiled. "My prescription still applies. Keep having fun. Live a little." Her smile turned distinctly naughty. "I also prescribe plenty of kissing. I'm," her doctor touched a hand to her chest, "giving you permission."

Ana felt her jaw drop, as in, right open. She finally got herself together enough to close her mouth. She swallowed hard. "Kissing?" Ana laughed. "You can't prescribe kisses."

Her therapist shrugged. "I can and I have. Go out on another date with this man," her eyes glinted, "this shifter, and let him kiss you."

"I had planned on seeing him again, but we agreed… I already told him no more kissing. Sure, little friendly pecks, but nothing hot enough to get the blood racing." She shook her head. "I doubt he'll even try." She was shocked to hear the disappointment in her voice

"Well…" Her therapist raised her brows, she leaned forward in her chair. "I guess that means you'll have to kiss him then."

Her mind was still in a blur when she left Doctor Brenner's office ten minutes later. She wasn't going to overthink this. Ana needed to take some control of the situation. So far, the ball had been firmly in Winston's court, maybe she should take some initiative. She had an idea. Ana pulled out her cellphone and texted Winston. It was the first time she had made contact with him. She typed out the message and pushed send before she could change her mind. His response was quick.

Sounds like a plan. Looking forward to it, and Ana, make it good. Fun is awesome… but interesting is better. Surprise the hell out of me.

What the hell had she done to herself?

CHAPTER 13

THREE WEEKS LATER...

Winston watched as Ana parked her car. He couldn't help but grin. It was probably goofy looking but he didn't care. He was happy to see her and really looking forward to their date. The words of her message played through his mind.

> *I'll organize our date for next time you're in town.*
> *Something fun, just like the doctor ordered.* ☺

Smiley face. For some reason he found it cute she had used one. Friendly and light-hearted. He fucking loved that she was taking the reins this time around. There was something sexy in that, especially since she was so timid about the whole dating thing. It was definitely good for her. This way she could control the situation.

They hadn't messaged again after that. He'd wanted to send her a little text here or there but he hadn't done it. He was afraid he might scare her off. Winston enjoyed her company. It was a pity there would be no more kissing, now that had been a serious treat. Ana had kissed him like her life depended on it. It had been hot and heavy from the start. His hands had itched to skim her curves but that would have been pushing the boundaries. Thing was, he didn't mind the thought of pushing the boundaries a little. Just a teeny, tiny bit. He didn't mind the thought at all. Unfortunately, Ana didn't feel the same. It was definitely one of her many attributes. She was attracted to him but didn't want him in that way. The kiss had scared the hell out of her. Maybe she would change her mind at some point about them taking the role-playing a little further. He sure as hell hoped so.

Ana gave a little wave. She gestured to the passenger seat in her car. A hatch-back. He waved back and then shook his head, pointing to his SUV. He was just playing with her. He didn't mind if they went in her vehicle.

Ana put down the window. "What's wrong? Look," she smiled, "I know you're used to fancy but—"

"It's not that," he chuckled. "I'm just not sure my legs will fit."

She pulled a face. What a cute face it was. Free from make-up, a smattering of freckles across the bridge of her button nose and her hair in a loose ponytail. He liked that she hadn't tried to be sexy. She was wearing a t-shirt. Something casual, that had been her brief to him. Casual with comfortable shoes. He wondered, and not for the first time that day, what was in store for him. For them.

She pursed her lovely lips. Her kissable lips. "Your legs will fit. You'll have to push the chair all the way back though."

Winston nodded. He walked over to the passenger side and made a show of trying to squeeze himself in. It wasn't as bad as he was making out.

Ana laughed. She gave his arm a slap. "Quit messing around and close the door already, time's-a-wasting." She paused. "It's good to see you, by the way."

"You too." Winston was still smiling like a crazy person when he found the lever to pull the seat back, next he adjusted the position of his legs and closed the door. Ana pushed the lock button and calmly waited for him to click his seatbelt in place before easing out of the parking lot. She wore little jean shorts and sandals. He caught a flash of color on her toenails. Looked like pink. Fuck but her legs were amazing. He forced himself to tear his gaze off of them. "And, are you going to tell me where we're going?"

She shook her head. "It's a surprise."

He couldn't argue with that. "Did you have a good month?"

"Great, thanks!"

"So," he rested his hands on his thighs, "how was work?" He glanced her way.

"All good. How are things... in shifter land?" She smiled, her concentration on the road ahead.

"Um..." he huffed out a breath.

"Uh oh! That doesn't sound good." She glanced his way.

"It's probably nothing but our game has been scarce lately."

"Game?" She frowned heavily.

"Yes. We normally have plenty herds of deer up and around the mountains where we live. Plenty of food."

Her eyes widened and she glanced at him and then back at the road a few times. "As in, you hunt?" She gave a nervous giggle. "I suppose you are a shifter, so... I guess it's normal, right?" She stopped for a red light.

He had to laugh at the way she was looking at him. "Yup, hunting is very normal for us, since we're part animal."

"Do you hunt in your—?" She licked her lips, trying to come up with the right words. "Your human form, or do you…" she hesitated.

"Shift into my wolf form?" he helped her out.

Ana nodded, "Yeah." Her eyes were wide with what looked like excitement. She pushed down on the gas and they continued out of town.

"We shift into our animal form. I'm a wolf shifter so I shift into my wolf form when hunting. It's easier that way."

"Oh wow… okay…" her words were breathy. "You just track them down and rip out their throats with your teeth?" She swallowed hard, glancing his way. There was still excitement laced in her words.

"Pretty much." He winced at what her reaction might be. "We need to eat."

She nodded vigorously. "I get it… I do. If you don't hunt, you don't eat."

"That's right. It's more than that though, we enjoy hunting as well. It's part of who we are."

"So the deer have been disappearing?" She raised her brows.

"Yup." It was his turn to frown. "They're becoming harder and harder to find. We're having to track the herds for days."

"Do you have any idea why?"

"None. We're clueless. We've always been really careful not to overhunt or to spook the herds. We don't go for pregnant females." He sighed. "It's not illness, we haven't seen any dead or sick animals. It's a mystery, one we have to find a solution to. We're shifters, we like eating meat. Right now we're on rations and on the verge of having to bring in nuts and soybeans." He made a choking noise. "Eating rabbit food is not in our DNA."

"I'll bet." She smiled. "Hopefully you'll find out what's going on soon."

"I hope so too. We're sending out extra scouting parties. There's something going on and it's only a matter of time before we figure it out."

"How weird and mysterious. It'll probably be something really stupid in the end."

"That's what I keep saying. My friend, Ash, is convinced that it's something more sinister, but let's hope you're right." They were headed out of town. "You're either kidnapping me... or, we're going away for the night on a camping trip?" The idea appealed to him in ways that it shouldn't. The thought of sharing a little two-man tent was enticing. Not they would do anything. It was just the idea of spending time with her, of sleeping with her... just sleeping. It appealed to him big time.

"No, nothing quite that exciting. You're making me wish I had thought of it though." She chewed her lower lip like maybe she had thought about it, but had decided against. *Pity!*

"How have you been this month? What did your therapist say? Any new prescribed advice?" *Stop with the twenty questions!*

She shook her head, her cheeks looking redder and redder by the second. "I've had a good month. All good!"

Winston chuckled. "No really, what did she say?" Then it dawned on him why she was acting so strangely.

"You told her about the kiss, didn't you?"

Bingo! Her cheeks went a bright red. Made him wish he had marshmallows. If he brought them to her face they would melt for sure.

"No." She shrugged, trying to look indifferent. "Not at all."

Such bullshit! Winston laughed. "Yeah, right. You told her about the kiss but for some reason you don't want to admit it." He looked at her pointedly.

Ana kept her gaze facing forward and shook her head, turning onto a dirt road.

"What did she say then?" he asked, jostling about in his seat as they headed further and further down the bumpy road.

"She's happy with my progress." Her eyes still firmly on the road ahead. There was more. Oh, most definitely more, but he decided not to push.

"Pretty isn't it?" Ana said as she turned a sharp corner.

He looked ahead of them, seeing a wide lake. It was picturesque with the mountains in the backdrop. That's where he lived, deep in those mountains. He'd seen the lake before but never from this angle.

"Sure is." He paused, his mind working. "We're going boating?" he guessed. There was a rowboat out on the lake.

She shook her head. "Stop! I didn't think up something that amazing. It's not camping or boating."

"Swimming? I wouldn't mind a little dip."

"Did I tell you to pack a suit?" She looked at him for a second or two before looking back at the road.

"Who needs one?"

Her cheeks turned distinctly red, all over again. "No

swimming or boating, we're going fishing." She smiled broadly. "I haven't been fishing in years and years, not since I was a little girl. My dad used to take my brother and me all the time. Do you fish?"

Winston nodded. "Absolutely, but I prefer to use my claws for that as well."

"No claws." She looked a little shell-shocked. "You might scare off the locals."

He laughed. "Oh, fuck, they would crap themselves. My wolf is much bigger than a normal everyday wolf. About three times the size."

Her eyes widened. "Really?"

"Would it scare you, if I shifted?" His voice held a timid edge. He would hate to scare this female. Not that he planned on shifting or anything.

An easy smile took hold of her mouth. "Not at all. I feel really safe with you. I'm sure I would feel the same about your wolf form, I mean," she paused, "it's just another part of you, right?"

He pushed out a breath through his nose. "Exactly… it would still be me inside."

She parked at an open spot. There were some males fishing a couple of hundred yards to their right. Ana turned to look at him. "Your eyes are exactly like I would picture the eyes on a wolf being." She looked from one to the other.

"That's because I am part wolf. I'm glad you feel safe with me, because you are… you're very safe." He clapped his hands on his thighs. "I'm excited about fishing. I've never had to catch them with a rod and reel. I've never had to catch anything like humans do. I take it as a challenge. It can't be that difficult."

"I don't know, I remember it being quite challenging

at times." They got out of the car. "You need to know what you're doing and I'm bound to be really rusty." Ana headed for the trunk, which she opened.

It was packed with everything from the fishing poles to fold-up chairs, as well as a picnic basket. He could scent delicious things inside.

"Also," she wrinkled up her nose, looking disgusted, "worms are the best bait."

He hefted a couple of items out of the trunk. "By the look on your face, I take it we don't have any or that I'm on bait duty?"

She shook her head. "We don't have any. I can't put innocent little worms on the end of our hooks. I just could not do it."

"I would have helped out with that, I—"

"No, I wouldn't have let you." Her eyes were wide. "It wouldn't be right."

"I just finished telling you how I hunt and kill deer and you don't want me to put a worm on the end of a hook?" He choked out a laugh.

"That's different. You hunt for food. This is for fun. We can't kill worms just so that we can have a bit of fun. No… just no." She shook her head vehemently.

Fuck but he liked this female. He seriously liked the hell out of her. "Are we, at least, fishing with actual sharp hooks or is there some other way of reeling them in?" He gave her his best shit-eating grin.

She huffed out a solid breath, her shoulders sagging. "No, unfortunately there was no way around that. We'll just have to be really careful when we take the hook out, I didn't buy the barbed kind so we have more chance of losing the fish. It'll make it more interesting though. I also bought a pair of pliers to make taking out the hook easy and efficient." She pointed at a packet.

He chuckled. "So, what bait are we using to fish with then?"

"Doughballs. They're apparently the best non-live bait that there is. I got the tutti-frutti and the vanilla flavor… fish must have a sweet tooth." She picked up the packet.

"Oh well, let's do this thing." He really was excited at the prospect of trying his hand at it.

It took an hour before the rods were set up. One for each of them. Another twenty minutes for Ana and a half an hour for him, before they got the hang of casting the things. Each time he cast, the line either got tangled or the bait didn't end up going out further than a few feet. "We should organize a boat next time," he said, putting his rod down onto the holder, eyes on his line in case he got a bite.

"Nah, boats are for cheaters." He heard her set her rod down as well.

"Says who?" He glanced her way.

She leaned back in her chair. Her t-shirt was baggy but she still managed to look really sexy. "My dad would say it, although I suspect it was because we couldn't afford to get a boat."

"So, what made you think of fishing in the first place?" He looked back at his line, sure he might have seen movement.

"I'm not sure you want to know right at this moment." She smiled.

"I think I do – your smile is distinctly naughty."

"No it is not!" She looked put out. "Now I definitely can't tell you."

"Come on! Just tell me already."

Ana adjusted the baseball cap she was wearing and sighed. "Fine! You asked for it. A guy came into the emergency room this week.

"You made your decision on where we were going to go based on an emergency room visit?"

She nodded. "I did."

"Go on," he said between chuckles.

That naughty smile was back. Her eyes glinted in the afternoon sun. "He'd been in a fishing accident."

"No, don't tell me…" He scrunched up his eyes. "Please don't tell me his dick got it." He cupped his member.

Ana laughed. "No, not his dick."

His cock gave a twitch as she said the word dick. The whole 'no sex' decision was making him horny like a teenager. It was amazing how interesting something became once it was banned, self-imposed or not. It didn't matter in the least.

"It wasn't his dick, but his left ball that got it." She shook her head and gave a low whistle. "That hook was buried in deep."

"Ah, fuck!" Any thoughts of sex vanished. *Thank claw!* Although Ana was sexy as anything, she was his friend. Thoughts of ripping off those little shorts were bad… very very bad, and not in a good way.

"Yup, and the hook was barbed. Seriously barbed. That sucker was stuck fast."

Winston made a groaning noise. "And this made you decide that fishing was what? A good idea?"

"I… um… I didn't choose the barbed hooks. I did that especially…" She nodded, her ponytail bobbed in time with her head.

"You did that for the fish, not for my balls." He

widened his eyes, choking out a laugh. His hand cupped more protectively around his cock.

"I think you're going to be just fine." Her eyes drifted down to where his hand held himself. A flash of… hunger crossed her face. If he had blinked, he would have missed it. A bolt of desire shot right through him, tightening his groin.

Then her eyes widened and her mouth dropped open. Ana pointed. "Your rod, your line… fish… You have a bite!" She screamed the last, jumping to her feet.

Winston grabbed his rod. Not too hard or he'd rip the hook clean out of the fish's mouth. He held his breath. There was a light tugging feeling on the end of the line. "I have him… it… I feel it there!" he yelled, taking hold of the reel. "What do I do?" he shouted, looking at Ana and then back at the line which moved through the water. There was definitely a fish on the end of it.

"Slowly lower your rod as you wind."

He did as she said.

"Slow and easy… not too fast," she added, her voice elevated.

He slowed down.

"Yes, that's it. Now, stop reeling and lift your rod back up. Not too heavy-handed or you'll lose the fish." She walked over to him. "Now reel… slowly!" she yelled. "This isn't a race, it's a dance."

"Something else your dad says?"

She exhaled. "Yeah." He could hear she was smiling.

One second there was a tugging on the end of the line and the next it was gone. His hand even fell back a few inches as the line gave. "What the…?" He reeled. *Nope!* He couldn't feel anything there anymore. "I think I lost him." He reeled some more, lifted the rod. "Yip," he sighed, "I lost him. I'm not sure what happened." He began reeling in earnest. Within seconds, his gleaming hook appeared. *No fish! No bait!*

"The little shit," he muttered.

Ana laughed. "You need to take it slow." She moved back to her own rod. "Better luck next time."

"At least we know that there are fish in this lake."

"Oh, they're in there alright." He could hear that she was smiling.

Almost an hour later and Ana hit a hand against her thigh in frustration. "Dammit!" she yelled. "I almost had him." The next two bites had been Ana's but she'd lost the fish both times in much the same way as Winston had.

"You need to take it just a little bit slower." He threw her words back at her. "It's a dance, not a race."

She rolled her eyes and shook her head. "You're full of shit."

"Better luck next time." He winked at her.

Ana pushed out a laugh.

He took a sip of his beer. "I think you screwed us with the non-barbed hooks. These fish are having a field day down there. Laughing their fins off at us."

She narrowed her eyes at him, looking serious. "You can tease all you want but your balls and your cock are thanking me right now."

Fuck! There it was again, another zing of need coursed through him. His balls and his dick could think of ways of thanking Ana. Lots of ways. Shit! He was getting hard and needed to stop this chain of thought right fucking now. One that involved his dick inside her and his balls slapping against her. Ones that involved making her come… multiple times. *Ana is vulnerable. She's your friend, asshole!*

"You have one!" she yelled, tossing her rod on the ground. The rebaiting of her hook completely forgotten.

He was saved by another scaly bugger and this time he planned on catching the thing. There would be no more laughing at them – no more! He reeled… slowly. He lifted the rod… carefully. He reeled some more… infinitely carefully. Closer and closer and closer. He caught a ripple at the surface. Closer still, and then a fin… right there, it was right there and then… bam! The hook came out. The little smooth fucker popped right out. As if to mock him. No, not as if – the scaly fuck was definitely mocking him when it leapt clear out of the water.

No way.

Not a fuck.

Without thinking, Winston leapt into the water. Three seconds later he held his prize above his head with a roar of triumph. "You are mine!" he growled. "Mine!"

"No!" Ana shouted. "Please no," she added.

He felt himself frown. *Why did she look so distraught?* He lowered the fish, looking the thing over. It was a decent size and… splash! She spluttered as she surfaced, her eyes wide. Then she coughed a couple of times. "Don't you even think about it," she managed to get out. Ana was drenched, from her cute ponytail to the lovely sandals on her feet.

She wiped a hand across her face. "Don't kill the poor thing! It didn't do anything to you." Her eyes were on the fish.

Winston bit back a laugh. "Is that why you just leapt head-first into the water, to save the little fish from the big, bad wolf?"

"You're mocking me." She put her hands on her hips and looked him in the eyes. Hers narrowed.

"Nope, not at all." He put the fish into the water and let it go, washing his hands in the cool water. *Not looking! Not fucking looking at how her shirt is molding her breasts right now. Not looking at how tight her nipples are. How fucking lush... no!* "I wanted to catch that fish... I would never have killed it. Not today anyway."

She pushed out a pent-up breath. "I thought your instincts took over. The way you roared like that and all that growly business... I really thought you wanted to kill the poor thing. I've never seen someone move so fast before."

"You were impressed." He bobbed his brows. "Admit it."

She stuck her tongue out at him. "So damned full of it."

"I told you we'd take a dip." He laughed. "And look, I managed to get you wet."

Wet.

Fuck! He hadn't just said that. By the way her pupils dilated, he could tell Ana's mind had wandered straight below the belt, just as his had. Even though he hadn't meant it like that, at least to begin with.

Heat pulsated between them despite the cold water. In order to try and defuse the situation, he hoisted her up. Ana squealed but he could hear that she was smiling. Her body felt warm against his. *So damned soft.* He needed to stop thinking along those lines. Winston dunked them both. The water was so cold. He heard her sharp intake of breath as he stood back up, followed by a nervous giggle. Her arms tightened around him. "You asshole!"

"It's cold," he muttered.

"It's freezing." It sounded like her teeth were shattering.

He walked out, wading through the water, Ana still in his arms. Winston scanned their supplies. No towels, but there was a blanket. She shook in his arms as the air hit her dripping body.

Winston grabbed the blanket with one hand, putting Ana down first before wrapping her up in it. He ran his hands up and down her sides to try to instill warmth. He already felt much better despite being soaked to the bone.

Ana laughed. "I can't believe you just did that."

"I can't believe you thought I was going to kill that fish. That you jumped in to save it." He wrapped his arms around her, rubbing her back. She felt good in his arms.

She suddenly tensed. *Shit!* Had he overstepped the mark? "Are you okay?" Winston asked as he pulled back, keeping his hands on her upper arms.

"I'm fine."

She was not fine. He could see that her mind was working. "You sure?" He let her go completely.

Ana nodded. "It's just, you asked me earlier about what my therapist said when I told her about our kiss."

Winston folded his arms. "Yeah, and what did she say?"

"She said that it was good for me. She even prescribed more kisses." She looked somewhere over his shoulder as she said it. "And, not just small ones," she mumbled that last, her gaze moved to the ground.

"She did, did she?"

Ana made a sound of agreement. Despite the cold, her

cheeks looked flushed.

"What do you think about it?"

It took some effort for her to look him in the eyes. "I'm of two minds. I enjoyed the kiss, but we're friends. Friends don't kiss friends like that."

"It's just kissing though." *No biggie.* He shrugged.

He could see she was thinking it over, water still dripped down her face. Her hair was plastered to her scalp. "Yeah, I guess." Then she smiled. "We may not kiss like friends but we are – just friends that is."

"Definitely." He had a thought. "By the way, we're supposed to be fake dating right?"

"Yes, role-playing." She nodded.

"We shouldn't really mention that if we're trying to be authentic. We agreed last time remember? I'm pretty sure your therapist would agree." He wiped some water off of his face and raked his fingers through his dripping hair.

She looked thoughtful.

"We should be all in about it. Not mentioning that we're friends and that it's fake. We need to try to believe it's real, even though we know it's not. You can ask your therapist but I don't think she would approve of us talking about being just friends all the time."

"You're probably right. No more mention of it then. We'll pretend we're dating for real?"

He nodded. Ana looked at him and he looked at her, another flush of red crept up her neck, spilling over onto her cheeks.

"Maybe we should dive into that picnic basket," he finally said, even though the last thing he wanted right now was food.

"Good idea." She seemed relieved.

Ana wasn't wrong. Friends didn't kiss like they had. He wasn't wrong either though, it had just been a kiss, nothing more and nothing less. For whatever reason, Ana trusted him, she felt comfortable with him and he wasn't about to take advantage of that. He had said he would help her through her fears. Having said that, he could not cross that invisible line. It was not going to be easy though. That was for fucking sure.

CHAPTER 14

ONE MONTH LATER...

"**N**o fair," Ana yelped as she lost her footing... again. She'd lost count of how many times she'd lost her balance in the last hour and a half. Too many to count on one hand, maybe even both hands. It was slippery, dammit. Very slippery. She put her arms out, trying hard to regain her balance. Why the hell did she bother? Ana was about to fall so darned hard. It seemed like the ice was rushing up to meet her, but in slow motion.

Strong arms banded around her, just as she was about to hit, they whipped her upright. Once she caught her breath, she looked up. Winston was grinning broadly. He was loving every minute of this. *The bastard!* She had to smile back. He *had* caught her after all.

She couldn't help noticing that his arms were like steel around her, only much warmer than any metal could be. "Got you." He raised his brows, a wicked glint in his eyes.

"You lied to me. *You* are a terrible… horrible person." Her smile grew wider.

"What did I lie about?" There was a huskiness to his voice. She noticed he hadn't tried to let her go.

"You lied about never having skated before. You're like a pro or something." She was gripping his biceps for all she was worth, both hands full. Oh so very full of hard muscle. Ana could scent his woodsy, masculine smell. Her eyes dropped to his lips. She remembered how good they had felt against hers. So soft. The guy could kiss. It wasn't just that she had been kiss-starved or that her 'kiss-odar' was functioning at lower than normal levels. The guy could really kiss. She didn't have to be a frequent flyer of the Kissing Club to know that.

True to his word, he hadn't tried to kiss her after that toe-curling first kiss though, not so much as a peck on the cheek since. Even though she had told him that her therapist had okayed it. She found herself wishing she'd been more assertive when he had asked her if more kissing was what she had wanted as well. She had played that moment through her mind several times.

Yeah, I guess.

That's what she'd said when he asked how she felt about them kissing for real. There was nothing confident and assertive about the answer she had given. If he tried to kiss her, she was jumping right in. It was a big 'if' though. They had to try it again. Just to prove that they could do it without her having an attack. That was the only reason… and maybe because she missed it. She was kiss-starved. That much was true. Winston had been right, it was just a stupid kiss. She'd totally overreacted when she'd told him it couldn't happen again.

"I most definitely did not lie. This is my first time on

the ice." He shrugged his big shoulders. "I can't help it that I'm good at most things." He winked at her.

Ana stopped herself from rolling her eyes but only because she could just imagine all the things that Winston would be good at. Lifting heavy things… and… running… maybe even handling a vehicle or… lots of things… so, so many things. Not hot and steamy things though. *No.* She hadn't been having sexual thoughts, just then. *Not at all.*

He carefully released her. She was reluctant to let him go. Her jeans were already soaked through from all the falling. She was sure to have a good couple of bruises come morning. Ana pulled in a deep breath and slowly let him go. First one arm and then the other. "You've got this," Winston said. "You can't try to walk though. Ice doesn't allow that. You'll just land on that sexy ass."

Sexy.

Ass.

Her.

Winston had noticed her ass. Had liked it. *No, you fool!* It was just a saying. He was just being nice. *Shit!* He was talking… best she pay attention. Ana nodded her head.

"…and that's why you have to slide your feet from side to side like this." He demonstrated, making it look easy.

"Let's go ice-skating," she mimicked Winston. "It'll be fun. I should have known you would choose something like this for your turn at picking what we do."

"It *is* fun."

"It is for you. I'm wetter than wet." She pointed at her jeans. "I'm pretty sure my ass is black and blue.

His brow creased. "You are really wet." His eyes seemed to darken. He skated backwards a few feet.

Wet.

There was that word again. Why did it make her feel dirty and naughty? Her mind should not tumble straight into the gutter every time he said it. Mind on the task at hand. Ana battled to keep from falling even when she wasn't moving. Going forwards was almost impossible and here he was skating backwards. *Backwards!* "Show off!" she mumbled.

"Come to me." He gestured for her to move towards him using two fingers of one hand. His eyes were on her. "Like I showed you… slow and easy."

Ana licked her lips. "Okay—" One tiny step and she was falling again. This sucked. She yelped, bracing for impact.

Winston caught her before she could land. He moved so quickly that she barely registered his movement. She was breathing hard, Ana clenched his shirt with one hand and gripped his… *Oh god!* She was holding his ass. His really hard, oh so fine ass. "Sorry," her voice was shrill.

Winston chuckled.

"I'm so very sorry." Her eyes were wide, her feet splayed too far apart. She was hunched over, her face level with his belly… abs… Winston did not have a belly. He had abs, a washboard, like the old-fashioned metal ones. Hard and ribbed. His ass was meaty and so firm it was obscene. "I wish I could let go but I'm scared I'll fall. In fact, don't move or we've both had it."

He chuckled again. "I think you may have fallen, just then, on purpose."

"What?" Her voice was shrill.

"You wanted to grab my ass… get your hands all over me, so," he grinned, "you faked a fall. You may as well just admit it."

She swallowed thickly. "That's not true! I would never—"

"You do realize," his voice was deep, "this means that I'm allowed to get my hands on you right back."

"You can't be—" She squealed when he gripped her hips and pulled her upright. Her hand left his butt and moved upwards to his back. *Shit!* Even his back was muscular. How did a person get themselves a muscular back? *Wow!* She looked up. Winston was grinning. His dimples were all over the place. So darned sexy. *The asshole.* He was mocking her. Her hand still felt warm from where it had been just moments ago. *Oh god!*

"I'm so sorry," Ana blurted. Her cheeks were so hot that she was surprised the ice beneath them wasn't melting.

He narrowed his eyes. "Maybe I should get myself a little off-balance." He wobbled, his skates slipping out from underneath him. Ana gave a yell as he scrambled to get himself… the both of them… back under control. At this rate, they were about to become a tangled heap on the cold, very wet ice.

A hand gripped her ass and she sucked in a breath, even made a little whimpering noise. His grip was firm. His hand hot through her wet jeans. Big and hot.

"There!" That grin of his was back. "Much better." The grin morphed into a smirk.

A laugh was pulled from her. "You're too damned much. I didn't grab your ass on purpose."

Winston seemed to think on it for a few seconds. "I don't know… I think you did. It felt like you did. Even if it was a… 'mistake'…" He said it like he didn't believe it. "I know you liked it."

Ana gasped. "Take that back. We're friends, I would never—"

"Friends don't date friends." He winked at her. They had agreed that when they were together they wouldn't talk about the whole fake dating thing, or about being just friends. Doctor Brenner had agreed that role-playing worked best when both parties committed themselves. When the pretense was as real as possible.

Then she remembered what he had said earlier. *The nerve!*

Ana gave a small nod of acknowledgment about the friend thing. After that, it was game on. "I didn't grab your ass on purpose. It was to keep from falling, but," she licked her lips, "since you totally grabbed mine on purpose—"

"You'd better believe it." He winked.

Ana shook her head, trying not to laugh. "I feel the need to make things even." Using a resolve she didn't even know she possessed, Ana gripped his ass. One butt cheek in each hand.

Winston's jaw tightened and for a second she thought that he might be angry. Maybe she had taken things a little too far. Then his mouth twitched like he was fighting a laugh. "Two hands? You're using two. That's not really fair now is it?"

His hand on her hip relaxed.

"I figure that two of my hands equal one of yours," she threw back at him.

He nodded. "I guess you might be right." Winston looked at her mouth and she realized how close they were. Her chest was flush against his.

His eyes moved back to hers. "I'm going to kiss you now, Ana."

"I'm struggling to breathe." It felt like the air had thinned. "My heart is racing as well." *Shit!* Was she about to have an attack... right now?

"Yeah, and your cheeks are flushed." His eyes glinted.

"I know, what if—?"

"It's perfectly normal though." Winston leaned forward, slanting his mouth across hers. *Soft, warm... so good.* He pulled away. "My heart is racing as well." Come to think of it, his breathing was also a little labored.

The hand on her ass tightened its hold, squeezing her flesh. She felt his touch right between her legs, in the form of a zing of lust. Ana moaned. To her horror, the sound was laced with need. *Oh shit! Oh no!* She sounded like a desperate hussy.

"Oh..." She felt her eyes widen. She let go of his butt. What the hell had she been thinking? "That didn't come out right. I didn't mean it to sound like that, I..."

"It's perfectly normal."

"It is?" What was Winston talking about?

"You're a female and I'm a male." He shrugged like it was no biggie. "I'm attracted to you and you're attracted to me."

"Yeah, no, I..."

Winston rolled his eyes, somehow managing to make that look sexy. He nodded. "Yes, you are. It doesn't mean we're going to act on it – I mean *really* act on it. We're having fun and enjoying each other's company."

She nodded. "It's not a big deal if we're attracted to one another? It doesn't mean anything?"

"That's what I said."

"Yeah." She nodded.

"It's not even weird that I'm going to go back to my room later and..." He bit down on his bottom lip. Then he huffed out a breath. "Never mind."

"What?" she asked. There was something about the look in his eyes, the way he bit down on his lip that had her blood rushing through her veins. "What are you going to do when you go back to your room?" Although she could guess, like a sadistic maniac, she needed to hear him say it.

"You don't want to know." His eyes seemed to darken. He pushed his lips together and breathed out of his nose.

"Oh, but I do." She sounded all breathless. She shouldn't be pushing this but she wanted to know. Had to know.

He leaned in close, his mouth right next to her ear. "I'm going to make myself come so damned hard just thinking about that moan."

She tried to hold back the gasp and failed. Even that sounded desperate and horny.

"I have needs," Winston went on. "Just because I'm not having sex doesn't mean I'm not getting off… getting myself off."

"I've become an expert in that." *Oh flip!* What the hell was wrong with her? She hadn't just said that! Ana squeezed her eyes shut. Maybe he had shared with her, but that didn't automatically mean that she needed to share with him as well.

"Four years is a long time."

"Very long. Infinitely long. So long that I've become somewhat of an expert in making myself come," she expanded on her earlier statement, her eyes were still shut. She cracked them open. What was wrong with her? What possessed her to say that as well? There was sharing and then there was oversharing.

Winston's nostrils were flared. He was breathing deeply. "You need to tell me… I really need to know, do you use one of those human vibrating devices or," his voice was low and deep, "do you use your hand?"

Flip! She was breathing deeply as well. "My hand," she whispered. She'd said so much already, may as well go the whole damned hog.

He groaned. "I knew it."

"We shouldn't be talking about this. It… it doesn't seem right." She was still holding his ass with both her hands. He was still squeezing her left butt cheek in his.

"You're probably right." He sounded disappointed. "Although, masturbation is a perfectly normal thing. You know that, don't you?"

Ana made a sound of acknowledgment as she slid her hands onto his hips. There, that was better.

Winston let go of her ass as well. Then he released her completely. She made herself do the same and she nearly fell, scrambling to stay upright. He chuckled, grabbing hold of her again… this time, he held her arms. "I'm going to let go of you and you're going to skate to me again."

"I think that maybe I'm done."

"I'm going to teach you how to skate, even if it's the last thing I do."

"Why?" she wailed, "it's not like it's a skill I'm ever going to need."

"You never know." He let go of her and she managed to somehow keep her balance.

Winston skated backwards. He gave a 'come hither' hand gesture. This time, Ana skated two whole steps before losing her balance.

Just as before, Winston was there in an instant, only

this time, she was too far gone. Her boobs even brushed the ice. Winston growled as he hoisted her, his skates going out from under him as well. Not only was she going to fall but he was going to fall on top of her. She was about to be really cold and really squashed. Like a frozen pancake.

Instead of landing on the ice, face down, she experienced a moment of suspension, her stomach gave a lurch as it felt like it was being pulled from her body. Ana landed on something warm. Unyielding, although not nearly as hard as the ice.

Her face was right next to his, their breath mingled. She was chest-to-chest and cheek-to-cheek with Winston. She was straddling his big body. Her body reacted. Ana reminded herself Winston was a guy and that she was a woman. It was perfectly normal.

"Your heart is racing." Winston's chest rumbled against hers as he spoke.

"Yup," a whisper.

"Your breathing is faster," another deep rumble.

"Yes."

He clasped her upper arms and pulled her away slightly, making them almost nose-to-nose. "Just as I thought." A sexy half-smile appeared on his lips. His beautiful lips. "Your cheeks are flushed."

"They are?"

He nodded. "Are you having a panic attack?"

She gave the smallest shake of the head, unable to take her eyes off of his. "I don't think so."

"Good." He crushed his mouth to hers. His hands moved over onto her back, pulling her closer to him. The kiss was not as hard and fast as the first one had been. It was softer, more languid and in many ways even hotter.

It felt intimate somehow, his tongue mimicking the act of lovemaking. She whimpered, her eyes closed, her toes curled as much as ice-skates would allow. He groaned into her mouth, his chest vibrating against her. Her nipples hardened. A perfectly normal and natural reaction.

Winston cupped her cheeks and broke the kiss. He pecked her lips before smiling at her. She grinned back. Doctor Brenner was right. Kissing was fantastic. She loved it, wanted more of the same.

Whose stupid idea was this dumb movie in the first place?

Ana squirmed in her seat. The scent of her arousal hit him, causing his already hard dick to harden up a whole lot more. His cock throbbed behind his zipper.

"Maybe we should watch something else?" His voice was so guttural that he cleared his throat, trying hard to dislodge the lust that threatened to choke him.

"We're both adults." Ana's gaze was locked on the screen. Her chest rose and fell in quick succession.

They'd picked up a comedy. A fucking romantic comedy. Was this kind of sex scene normal for a comedy? The female onscreen bounced on the guy's dick. She threw her head back and wailed, breasts bouncing hard. *When is it ever going to end?* On and on she bounced, wailing louder and louder. Thing was, Winston was aroused by Ana's arousal, not by what was on the screen. All he could think of was sucking on her clit and making her come using both his mouth and his dick. What hot-blooded male wouldn't have these kinds of thoughts? *A decent one.* A *good* male wouldn't be picturing Ana bouncing on the end of his own dick like Winston was doing right now. Her long hair loose and flowing, her face drawn in ecstasy.

"Thing is…" Shit, his voice was still ridiculously deep. "We're both in a dry spell at the moment and… fuck…" It was his turn to squirm. His dick physically hurt. He reached for a pillow. They'd kicked some of the extra scatter cushions on the floor. Winston placed the pillow firmly on his lap and turned back to Ana. Her eyes were wide and on the pillow. *Shit!* She'd seen his bulging cock. The denim ready to rip. "Sorry."

She swallowed deeply. "No, that's alright. So you like them busty, I guess?" Her voice was soft.

They both turned back to the screen as the female screeched, her eyes scrunched shut.

"Finally," Winston huffed. "That male is shit in bed. Absolutely clueless. Oh look…" He waved a hand in the general direction of the television and made a noise of disgust.

"What's wrong?"

"They're cuddling," he said in a shocked tone.

"What's wrong with cuddling? I mean, I know shifters aren't looking for love or anything but cuddling is normal after sex." She was frowning heavily.

He had to laugh. "That's not what I mean. He gave her one measly orgasm – or should I say, she *took* one orgasm because that douche *gave* her jack shit."

"One measly orgasm as opposed to…?"

Was she for real? Then again, she hadn't been with anyone in years. "As opposed to a string of orgasms. One is never enough. He also just laid there and made her do all the work. Just folded his hands behind his neck and that was it. The jerk doesn't deserve to have a dick or to call himself a male."

"What should he have done then?"

Now she was taking the piss. He looked over at her. Ana looked completely serious. "Palmed her tits. Rubbed on her clit… stuck his thumb up her ass… fucked her back… something. As soon as she was done, he should have taken over and made her come again, only this time, much harder. Look," he waved at the screen, "she's still talking. She shouldn't be capable of speech."

Ana burst out laughing. She clapped a hand over her mouth. Her eyes were wide. She looked shell-shocked, excited and embarrassed all at once. "You're joking about the whole ass thing right? And about not being able to talk?"

"No, I'm deadly serious. You have no idea how much harder you come if—" He pressed down on the pillow. "Would you mind passing the popcorn?" Now he wanted to show her. Explain with his hands, his dick and his mouth exactly how sex should be. It would explain why females lined up on Shifter Night and why he had sworn off females in the first place. There was no way he could do it though. Ana was his friend and he had made a promise to wait.

Ana handed him the bowl. "I guess you're pretty experienced since you've had so many different partners."

"Yeah." He shrugged. "I picked the older females in the early days. Females who knew what they wanted and weren't afraid to demand it and to give plenty of feedback. I learned the ropes quickly."

"I'm sure you did, Mr I'm-good-at-most-things."

She was picking up on his tension and trying to take it easy on him. "I'm not proud of all the females I've slept with. I don't care if I have to wait years for my name to come up… no more." They both sat in silence for a few moments. "What about you? I'm sure you had males lined up wanting to take you out. Hell, I'm sure they still try their asses off."

She shook her head. "Nah! I've only ever been with two guys. The first one was a big mistake and the second one…" She let the sentence die.

"Was special?" he finished for her. *Fuck!* She'd only ever been with two males. *Two.*

"He was very special."

"Was it John?"

Winston watched her shut down. *Shit!* He should never have asked her that. He knew the answer.

She finally nodded once. "Yes, it was John, but I don't really want to talk about it. I'm enjoying myself. I'm finally making some progress and," she shrugged, "I guess I want it to continue."

Winston nodded. He reached over and squeezed her hand. Both of them refocused on the movie. Winston picked up another handful of popcorn. He dropped it back into the bowl. "Let's order some Chinese." The couple onscreen were about to go at it again. This time in the shower. Winston clicked the pause button. "We'll watch that psychological thriller, if you don't mind?" Thank fuck they'd rented two movies.

"I don't mind. I just can't believe you want more food?" Ana raised her brows. "We just ate not long ago."

He nodded. "I have a high metabolism. You should know that by now."

She laughed. "You're right, but you still manage to surprise me more often than not. I suppose I could do with a couple of egg rolls." Ana was still smiling.

Winston got up. "Great!" He walked towards the

kitchen, she kept the take-out menus in the top drawer. "Oh, and Ana….?" He turned back.

"Yeah?" She had her legs tucked underneath her on the sofa. Her hair was loose about her shoulders. *Fucking beautiful.*

"It's the whole package – eyes, hair, body, personality – all of it. It's everything about a female. Not just her ass or her… chest. So, just because that female had big breasts, does not mean I was attracted to her."

"Oh, okay. I just thought that because you were… you know… that you were turned on by Jennifer Wilson."

"Who the hell is Jennifer Wilson?" He frowned, taking a step back into the room towards her.

"The actress in that movie, the one with the big…" She held her hands out over her chest. "Men love her."

"I couldn't give two shits about Jennifer Wilson. My hard-on had nothing to do with what was happening onscreen." He was saying too much. "Don't take this the wrong way but you're beautiful, Ana, and you give off the most amazing scent when you're turned on. My body sometimes forgets that we're friends. Don't worry though because I haven't. I respect you."

Her eyes turned a bit glassy and she blinked a couple of times. "That's so incredibly sweet. Thank you! I appreciate you spending time with me. I'm really enjoying myself. I've almost stopped worrying about having a panic attack. You're a really good guy." She looked down at the floor. "I guess I really miss sex, that's all. So, if I make stupid noises while we're kissing or I give off that scent you're talking about, it's not personal or anything."

Ouch! His ego took a bruising but at the same time, it was exactly what he needed to hear. "I know. It's fine."

"And I respect you too."

Double fucking ouch! Winston nodded. Oh well, he had said it first and he had meant it. "Let me fetch that menu."

She smiled. "Do you think I'll get over this... whatever is holding me back?"

Yes, he did. Big time yes. He should probably take her straight to the Dark Horse right now, but he couldn't. He was a selfish fuck because he wasn't done spending time with her yet. One or two more weekends and then he'd have to do the right thing by her even if it killed him.

"You're looking at me funny. I take it you think I'm a lost cause? That I'll be fifty and married to my dildo?"

"You have no fucking idea how wrong you are on both counts. I think you're going to be just fine. A few more dates with me," he winked at her, "and you'll be ready."

"You really think so?" She smiled. "I don't feel as nervous at the prospect of meeting new people."

"See!" He raised his brows. "I really do think you'll be ready." He felt himself frown. "I thought you said you didn't use a dildo though." *Fuck!* His voice was husky again.

"Just because I use my hand doesn't mean I don't own a dildo."

Winston nodded. He leaned against the doorjamb. "Have you thought about what you plan to do when you do start dating again? Are you going to try the internet again or...?"

Ana shook her head. "No way. That was awful. I was thinking I should have sex first. Just get that out of the way like we did with our first kiss..." Her eyes widened. "Not that I meant that we should... you know..."

"Fuck." Her eyes widened as he said it.

"Yes, that." Her voice was husky as well.

"Say it." He smiled.

"Why?" She folded her arms.

"How are you going to do it if you can't even say it?"

She pushed out a breath. "I suppose you're right." Ana didn't say it though, she just sat there.

"You've only had sex with two people, you're not one for fucking around, which is a good thing. You should forget about having casual sex. I promise you, it's not all it's cracked up to be."

"Fuck." She widened her eyes and grinned. "There, I said it. Fuck, fuck, fuck," she giggled, looking happy with herself.

His dick loved hearing her say it. His cock was perverted as hell, it started to harden.

"I can't start dating again – properly I mean – until I've had sex. I'll consider myself mostly cured after spending the night with someone." She lifted her eyes in thought. Like she was considering confiding in him. Then, her beautiful blue orbs locked with his. "I'm more fearful of starting a relationship than what I am of having sex. I know that sounds stupid, but it's true. Sex would be the next logical step."

"Are you sure that's what you want?" He wasn't sure why he was pushing this. The agreement was that they would fake date until she was able to meet people herself. This was all about desensitizing Ana and about them having fun. "You do know that if you find the right guy he'll be patient and kind. He won't mind if you have a panic attack. He'll hold your hand through the whole thing. He'll be the one to call the emergency services. He certainly won't mind a bit of puke on his shoe."

Ana's shoulders tensed, her jaw tightened. Her eyes took on a look of fear. Then she shook her head. "I'm not looking for a relationship. I thought I was, but I'm not ready. A guy like you described would only scare me off even more." She shook her head again. "This has got to be done in steps and the next logical step is sex. Since you're not available," she giggled, but it came out sounding nervous, "I need to find someone else – when the time comes, that is."

Fuck! He wanted to volunteer so badly. He grabbed the top of the doorjamb and squeezed. The wood creaked so he let go. "Okay, let me know when you're ready and I'll introduce you to a couple of the guys." His voice took on a hard edge.

She nodded. "Although, I'm not sure I'll ever feel ready. You might have to give me a push in the right direction."

"That's not for me to decide." He shook his head. There was no way he was handing her over to someone, or talking her into it. He wasn't her goddamn pimp. *Fuck!* "I still think it's a bad idea."

"Please, promise me, when you think I'm ready, even if I'm not sure myself, that you'll tell me. That you'll help me. It's what I need." Her eyes were wide and pleading.

"Okay." Winston looked into Ana's eyes. She was so damned sweet that it floored him. There was no way he could say no. Not all of the shifters were understanding males. None of them was good enough for her, but hell, he'd find the best possible male for the job, so help him.

"So, you'll introduce me and be there in case anything goes wrong?"

"No way, some of the males are into threesomes, but—"

"No, I don't mean that!" She looked at him like he had grown a tail or something. "I know you're saving yourself for when you hit the top of the list. I would never expect…" She sighed.

"Okay, okay!" He put up his hands. "Sorry, it's just that for a second there you sounded like you wanted me to be there, as in, in the room." The thought made him break out in a sweat. There was no way he could watch her with another male. Not a fucking chance.

"No, silly!" She looked like she wanted to say something and thought better of it. "Just that you'll be there at the bar with me. With us, at least until I'm comfortable."

"What are friends for?"

She smiled. It was radiant. "Thank you."

"You should probably start using that dildo," he blurted.

Her mouth fell open. "What? Why?"

"Preparation. Shifters are big… everywhere and you haven't had sex in a long time."

She swallowed hard. "Yeah. Okay… yeah." That scent of her arousal was back.

Winston tried to breathe through his mouth. Fuck, he could taste Ana. He turned, hoping she didn't catch a glimpse of his hardening dick. At this rate he'd have a permanent zipper indentation if he wasn't careful.

Yup, one or two more weekends and he'd give her that push she needed. He couldn't hold her back just because he loved spending time with her. It would be wrong.

CHAPTER 15

S omething wasn't right. He thought back to how Ash had acted so strangely a couple of months ago. How he'd sniffed the air and gouged the earth with his enormous clawed paws. It was a prickling sensation. Like he was being watched. It was a shift in the air. Not something he could get the scent of or a handle on. Just a feeling of things not being quite right.

"What is it?" his alpha asked, once the male completed his shift. Obviously Ward did not feel whatever it was that Winston was feeling. He didn't have that same sense of apprehension. That same feeling of foreboding, or the male would never have shifted. It was the same as last time where Ash had picked up on something but he hadn't.

Winston put his snout in the air and sniffed hard. He couldn't bring himself to don his human skin. To do so would mean showing weakness. Instead, his lip peeled back and a low growl erupted from somewhere deep inside him. His alpha would understand its meaning.

Beware.

Danger.

His skin prickled beneath his fur, which bristled. A need to scout their immediate surroundings took hold of him. Winston rushed forward, senses on high alert. He headed a hundred feet to the north-west and then another fifty to the east. He continued on, until he'd moved in a complete circle, back where he'd started.

Ward chuckled from somewhere behind him. He could hear the male walking towards him. Could hear each footfall on the soft earth. Could hear the odd snap of a pine needle.

"What's got you so rattled?" his alpha asked, about fifty feet away now.

They had been out there for two days. Far out. About a day's walk from home. Tracking game. If they went too much further, they wouldn't get their catch back home before it spoiled. His heart slowed its race and his breathing calmed.

Fuck!

Ash and his damned paranoia had spread over to him. He needed to give the male a piece of his mind when they got back to the village. Ash might be stronger but Winston was way faster, a ton more flexible.

A roar sounded behind him followed by a thud. *What the fuck?* Ward! His hackles went up. Winston did a one-eighty in mid-air. Jumping fallen trees and crashing through the undergrowth, Winston closed the distance between himself and his alpha within a second or two.

Ward lay face down, his back a torn up, bleeding mess. Winston scanned the area. Everything in him bristled. Adrenaline coursed through him. Whatever had done this was nowhere in sight. No animal was capable of moving quickly enough to inflict this type of damage and leave before Winston could catch sight of them. Even more concerning was the lack of scent in the air.

He could hear himself sniffing and snorting, trying to catch a scent. Ice ran through his veins. Whatever had done this was strong, moved like a ghost and left no scent. He growled and snarled. Facing one way and then the other. Standing guard against a nameless, faceless foe. One thing was for fucking sure. Whoever had inflicted this damage to Ward had meant to do harm.

The big alpha stalked to the other side of the large room and then back again. "I fucking told you," Ash snarled. "What did I say?"

"I guess I owe you my right nut," Winston threw back. "I never said that I would sever it for you though, just that you could have it. I guess I'll have to tattoo your name across it. It's going to hurt like a bitch, but," he shrugged, "a bet is a bet."

Ash pulled a face like he was sick to his stomach. "Don't you fucking dare." He barked out an awful sounding laugh.

"This is no time for joking. You're sure there was no scent? No tracks? No sign of anything or anyone?" Ward's eyes were wide. "Are you sure you didn't miss something? A shadow? Any-fucking-thing?"

"I was there in two seconds flat. I saw nothing. Scented nothing." Winston shook his head. "Like I said, I stood over you for a good couple of minutes. I figured we were sitting ducks anyway if I stayed, and so I shifted and carried you to the nearest scouting party, three and a half hours' walk away."

"You regained consciousness soon after," Brock chimed in. One of his panther shifters gave a deep nod.

Jarred had been one of the scouts in that particular party. The one they had met up with.

"I didn't do this to myself. Fuck!" Ward looked back over his shoulder. His back was covered in newly-formed, pink scars. "I think it's safe to say that whatever did this has also spooked our game."

"And you're sure you didn't see anything? Didn't scent anything?" Ash asked, his eyes on Ward.

The wolf alpha shook his head, his eyes stormy. "I sensed something. I had just started to turn when *bam!*" He clapped his hands together.

"Did you roar or was it whatever did this to you?" Ash asked.

"I don't know." Ward had his eyes narrowed in thought. "It happened so quickly. It knocked me straight out."

"It was no fucking wonder," Winston growled. "Seven ribs snapped and your spinal cord severed. Your right lung was punctured. Lord knows what else was pulverized inside you."

"They did a number on you," Ash said simply.

"We have to redouble our efforts," Ward said. "Pull the scouting teams back. We need bigger numbers on each team. Two or three males will be sitting ducks. Most importantly we need to keep more males in the villages."

"Protect our females and our children." Ash grit his teeth.

Brock nodded. "Agreed. Protect our own." He looked pointedly at Winston. His dark eyes menacing. "You sure you didn't catch a flash of fur? A hint of... something? We have no idea what the fuck we're dealing with."

Winston shook his head. "Nothing. Whatever did this

was long gone by the time I arrived."

"In less than two seconds flat." Ward shook his head. They all sat in silence for a few moments. "How is that even possible?"

"We can't afford to lose so many males on the weekends." Ash looked at Brock and then at Ward.

"If we cancel Shifter Night, we might have all hell break loose," Brock said, running a hand through his hair.

"Cancelling it outright is a bit extreme. Perhaps we halve the number of males who usually go." Ward winced as he sat on the edge of the table. His back was still tender. Winston could still recall how worried he'd been when he'd first seen Ward. Whoever had done this could have taken his head. Both of their heads for that matter.

Brock nodded. "I think it's wise to bump up security at the villages. I'll call a general meeting so that we can address the packs."

Ward nodded. "Yes, it's important that everyone is informed, particularly the weak."

Ash growled, flashing a canine. His eyes were darker, his whole stance tense. Winston felt it too, adrenaline rushed through his veins.

"About Shifter Night," Jarred piped up. "How do we decide who goes and who stays? There might be fighting amongst the males."

"Draw straws," Ward snapped.

"We can ask for volunteers to stay and, if need be, we'll resort to having to draw straws," Ash said.

"Who in their right mind is going to volunteer?" Jarred chuckled. He quickly stopped when no one joined in.

"I volunteer." It hurt to say the words. All he could think about was Ana. How much he missed her. It was her turn to pick a date for them. He hoped she hadn't gone to too much trouble. *Fuck!*

"Me too." Ash didn't look too happy about it.

"Jarred volunteers as well." Brock looked at the male, daring him to deny it. "As do I."

"Great!" Ward stood up, the lingering pain he felt evident in his pinched face and tense jaw. "I am sure that many more will be just as generous."

"Let's get the word out and call that meeting, the sooner the better. Now," he smiled, "I had better get back to my mate. Stephany is not too happy with me at the moment. Nearly took my head off when I got home. Good thing I was already partially healed by then."

"She's just afraid," Ash said. "She could have lost you."

Ward nodded. "Yup, she won't let me out of her sight. Crapped on me from a dizzy height when I got home in that sorry state. You'd swear my getting injured was my fault."

"I take responsibility." Winston swallowed hard. "I should never have walked away like that."

"Bullshit!" Ward slapped him on the back. "You knew something was out there, I should have listened. Should have paid more attention. Don't beat yourself up."

Winston nodded.

One by one the males trickled out of the room, leaving just him and Ash. Winston couldn't believe he wasn't going into town this weekend. He had been so looking forward to it. Ever since he met Ana he'd had a real reason to go into town. Something so much more than sex. Again he hoped she hadn't gone to too much trouble planning something special. He needed to give her a call to explain things.

"Hey," Ash said, still in the room. Winston hadn't even noticed, he'd been so deep in his own thoughts. "You look like you just heard the worst news in the…" Ash faltered. "Oh, I get it! You're upset you won't be seeing your female this weekend."

"Ana's not mine." Winston shook his head. "But yes, I guess I'm bummed I won't be going into town. I was looking forward to seeing her." He tried to play it down but Ash wasn't buying it. He cocked his head and raised his brows. He got this weird look on his face, like he was sizing Winston up.

"What? Just because I'm a little disappointed doesn't mean anything. Ana and I are friends."

"Savannah and I started out as friends. Did you know that?" Ash got that pained look he always got when he spoke of his mate. It had been three and a half years since she had died and you would swear it was yesterday.

"No, I didn't know."

"Well, we did, but before we knew it, things started getting a little heated. One thing led to another and before either of us realized it, we were in love. So fucking far gone it was insane. Seemed to happen overnight too." He got a faraway look.

"That's not what's happening with Ana." Winston pushed his hands into his pockets. "She sees me as just a friend. We even spoke a bit about it when I saw her last. She asked me to set her up with one of the males. She's not looking for a relationship." It was true and yet the words tasted bad on his tongue. He couldn't say why.

"I bet you love the idea of that right? Ana and another male?" Ash gave him a cocky as fuck grin. The male knew how much he hated the idea. It was easy to see. Winston only hoped Ana hadn't noticed.

It was just that Winston was worried about her. "Most of the males are nowhere near good enough for a female like Ana. She's sweet and kind and she's been through so damned much. She needs someone who's going to look after her. A male who's going to take it really slow. Someone who's very understanding. Most of our males are only interested in one thing and with so many willing humans..." He sighed and shook his head.

"So you need someone infinitely patient. Someone who will spend months with her if need be?" Ash folded his arms. "Someone more like... say... you?"

"Months might be pushing it a bit." He didn't like the idea of some male spending a ton of time with Ana. The two of them doing things together. Fun things. *No.*

Ash narrowed his eyes, seeming to look right through Winston. "You don't like the thought of her cozying up to another male?"

"That's not it," Winston quickly answered.

"I think I hit the nail right on the head." Ash winked at him.

"Hey, don't do that. That's not what I mean. It's not like that between us."

"So you keep saying. I think thou doth protest too fucking much! I suggest you watch it with that female. We're not permitted to date. Your name has not come up yet. It isn't likely to come up within the next few months. Hell, with the current crisis, it could take a whole hell of a lot longer. A year... years even. Things aren't safe around here for our females and children."

"I told you that it's not like that between us." Winston suddenly felt agitated. "I'm not even fucking her. What the hell are you talking about?" Winston pointed at Ash.

"Not fucking her." Ash squeezed his eyes closed for a few seconds like he couldn't believe what he was hearing. "What you're doing is ten times more dangerous. You're playing with fire and at this rate, you're liable to get burned. I suggest you fuck her or leave her. Actually, at this rate, I suggest you do both."

"I told you, I'm done with fucking around. Ana is special, there's no way I'm taking advantage of her in that way."

"But you'll hand her over to some other male."

"I hate the idea, okay? I'll admit it. I fucking hate the thought of some asshole with his hands all over her, but what else can I do?" Winston blurted. *What the hell? What? Fuck!*

"My point exactly." Ash huffed out a breath. "You're not going to be able to walk away if you allow this role-playing bullshit to go on. You definitely won't be able to just hand her over to some other male. I guarantee it."

"Of course I will." He meant it. He might hate it, but he would do it.

"How can you be so sure?" Ash shook his head. "I sure as hell wouldn't be able to do it."

"I will do it because it's what she needs. Ana is nowhere near ready to start a relationship with anyone right now, and even if she was, I'm not on that list. She does need to take things to the next level though, if she wants to get better. If it's what she really wants, and she told me that it is, then I'll help her. It's what friends do for one another."

Ash clasped him by the shoulder. "All I'm saying is be careful. You're going to get yourself hurt if you carry on like this. You're developing feelings for this female, I can tell," he spoke softly.

"I'll give it some thought."

"You do that." Ash's eyes had softened. He squeezed Winston's shoulder. "I'm here if you need to talk."

Winston nodded.

"I'll see you later." Ash released him and turned towards the door.

"Yeah," Winston said. "Later."

He told himself that there were a few things to prepare for the meeting and so he didn't call Ana right away. Then the meeting was held. It was only when the sun was long down and the packs were gearing up to have dinner that he finally got around to calling her.

It took a while for her to answer. "Winston." She sounded worried. "Is everything okay? Are you okay?" Very worried. He could hear different noises in the background.

"I'm fine. Where are you?"

She huffed out a breath. "Okay, flip, for a second there I was sure that something was really wrong. It's just that you've never called me before – you normally text. I just finished my shift at the hospital. I was on my way home, I had to pull over to answer the call. Are you still coming this weekend?" Her voice held an excited edge. "I have something cool planned. You'll love it. It involves food and a fun, and I know how much you love those things, especially the food."

Winston chuckled. "You know me well. Um…" He rubbed the back of his neck. "Something happened today and well…" Winston told her what had happened. The whole shebang. He told her about Ward going down.

"What?" Her voice was shrill. "Something attacked the person you were with? What do you mean something?"

"That's just it, we don't know. Remember I told you our game has been disappearing? Well, we think whatever did this is also responsible for spooking the herds."

"I don't like how you keep saying 'whatever' instead of 'whoever.'"

"*Whatever* did this isn't human, they can't be. They moved too quickly and quietly to be anything other than non-human. I don't know of any species like this. The weirdest thing was their lack of scent. It was creepy."

"You're freaking me out," Ana spoke quickly. "Are you sure you're okay?" He heard her swallow thickly. "Are you guys in danger right now? Is that what you're telling me?"

"Calm down." He smiled. "I'm back at the village. Ward is almost healed. We're all fine."

"It's just that I don't want anything to happen to you. You're my friend and I guess that means that I worry. I'm going to worry until you get here, at least it's only a couple of days."

Shit! Shit! Shit! "I can't come into town this weekend."

"What? Why not?" He could hear the disappointment in her voice.

"Whatever attacked Ward could be a threat to our village. We can't afford to lose so many males every Saturday night so we're cutting the numbers by half and bumping up security."

"That's means it'll be a whole month before you can come back into town." She sighed. "I understand though. You'd better text me, so that I know you're okay."

He chuckled. "I will. I'm bummed that I can't come through… I…" He sighed. "I miss you." There, it was out.

She laughed softly. "You just miss coming into town and all the fun things we do. You miss those steak rolls from the diner and the carnivore pizzas from Giovanni's."

"Nope." He paused. "I'm pretty sure I miss *you*." *Fuck!* Should he be saying this? Thing was, if he didn't see Ash for an extended period he would miss him as well. Not that he would ever tell the male. That would be weird. Ana was different though.

"Oh, okay…" she sounded skeptical. "Just stay safe. Promise me that you won't do anything stupid." Now she sounded mad. Was she mad at the prospect of him getting hurt or because he had said that he missed her?

"I'll be careful," he finally said when she didn't elaborate. "I'll text you every day."

"Every day," she laughed. "That's not necessary. Just let me know from time to time that you're still alive."

"Okay." Winston could hear the disappointment in his own voice.

"Stay safe and… we'll chat soon."

"Yeah." They said their goodbyes and he pushed the end button. It wasn't lost on him that she didn't tell him that she missed him back. Was Ash right? Was he developing feelings for her?

Fuck, maybe. The thought of not seeing her for another month didn't sit right with him. One thing was obvious to him though, Ana didn't feel anything beyond friendship. So, it didn't really matter. In fact, maybe it was a good thing that he couldn't go this weekend. It would give him some time to think things through.

CHAPTER 16

A na put down the phone and placed it back on the center console. She took a couple of deep breaths, checked for oncoming traffic and pulled out into the road. Her mind played through their conversation. *Oh god!* She pushed down on the brake pedal, realizing at the last second that the light was red. She had almost driven straight through the intersection. At this time of the evening, it was no longer all that busy, but there were still some cars on the road. Her vehicle screeched to a halt. She put her hand up as she glanced in the rearview mirror and mouthed 'sorry' to the driver behind her, who didn't look too impressed.

Her mind was all over the place. It hadn't meant anything when Winston had said that he missed her. He hadn't meant it like that. *What if he had though?* Her heart sped up. Her breathing increased tenfold. She put a hand to her chest. *Shit!* It felt like she was about to—The car behind her honked. He honked again, but Ana was too busy trying to breathe, trying to calm down, to take note. Then he sat on his horn.

She looked up, seeing that the light had turned green. *Damn!* That was quick. She put her hand up a second time. This time she got the bird. *Asshole!* At the same time, she couldn't blame him. She was blocking the road.

Her heart was still racing, her lungs inflating too quickly, so, to avoid causing an accident, she pulled over for a few moments.

Maybe she was just worried about Winston. *Sure, that's it.* She needed to think happy thoughts. Just because he said he missed her didn't mean that Winston had feelings for her beyond friendship. Everything was going to be okay. He was going to be okay. He was a shifter, he was strong. Ana swallowed hard. The shifters could protect themselves. Everything would be okay.

She leaned her head back against the seat rest and closed her eyes, focusing on slowing her breathing. She pictured wide open fields and glorious sunshine.

It did help, but she was still left with feelings of… anxiety. She grabbed her phone again and dialed Doctor Brenner's receptionist. Thankfully, she managed to get an appointment for the next morning.

⁂

Doctor Brenner nodded her head every so often while Ana took her through what had happened.

"Do you think that maybe your feelings for Winston have also gone beyond the bounds of friendship?" her therapist asked.

"I never said his feelings for me had changed… just that they *may* have. I don't know for sure though. I might be completely off the mark about that." She shrugged. "I'm probably wrong."

Doc Brenner nodded once. "Okay, I'll rephrase, do you think your feelings for Winston have changed? Have you started to see him as more than just a friend?"

"No… no way." She shook her head, wanting to deny it some more but she forced herself to keep her mouth shut.

"You're sure about that?"

Ana frowned. "Very sure. I'm nowhere near ready for a relationship. I didn't like it when he told me that he missed me. I just… I didn't like it."

"Why not?"

"He's my friend. I enjoy spending time with him. I'm improving because of him and I don't want that to stop. I don't want our friendship to end."

"And him having feelings for you would mean that you couldn't see him anymore?"

"That's right." She nodded. "I can't be friends with him if he wants more. It wouldn't work." She squirmed in her seat.

"Your friendship could evolve though, into more. It happens all the time. I'm reading a friends-to-lovers romance at the moment."

"Not this time!" Ana shook her head some more. "I'm not looking for a relationship and he's not allowed to be in one so, no, it wouldn't work."

"You do admit that you're attracted to him though?" Her doctor raised her brows.

"Yes," she moaned out the word. "I admit that I'm very attracted to him and he is just as attracted to me. We've openly admitted that. In fact," she pursed her lips together for a second, "you know I told him I was ready to take the next step. I asked him to introduce me to someone with the purpose of taking the next step."

"Sex?" Her therapist sat forward in her chair.

"Yeah, sex. It's been four years. I have to… go there

again some time. I have to at least try. I can't just give up. I have made progress and I think I might just be ready for that next step."

Doctor Brenner nodded.

"Winston has shown me that it could be possible, that I might just be able to do it. Thing is, I had planned to ask him if he would be willing to… help me out with that."

"Oooh, interesting. He said he wanted to wait though. No more sex until he found the right person."

"He said he was done with all the meaningless sex. Sex with me wouldn't be meaningless, would it? Am I being selfish here?" Ana made a noise of frustration. "I *am* being selfish. I made a joke about him and me… doing it and he ignored the insinuation flat out. It was wrong of me though." She wrung her hands together. "It doesn't matter anymore because I'm not so sure that's a good idea anyway. If there's even the slightest chance that Winston has feelings for me, us having sex would complicate things."

Her doctor cocked her head and narrowed her eyes. "I think you're right. Friends should not have sex with friends. It never works out. I'm not so sure that sex with a stranger is the answer either."

"Really?" Ana widened her eyes. "You told me to go out there and have fun… to keep stepping it up."

"Sex is huge though. It's ultimately up to you. If you feel that's what you need to do, then go for it. I'm not going to stop you. It's still a big step from where you are now though. You need to think long and hard before jumping into bed with someone." She sighed. "Also, be careful of where you're headed with Winston. It sounds like things could end up getting complicated."

Ana nodded. "Hopefully not. I don't want to lose his

friendship." She looked at Doctor Brenner skeptically. "I thought you said you wouldn't mind going to Shifter Night. Why the change of heart?"

"I'm not against a one-night stand per se. I've had a couple, and one or two were nights to remember. You're still really fragile though. One wrong move could put you right back. It's a bit of a catch twenty-two. I think Winston is good for you, but things change. They change before you know it."

"Winston and I *are* good. It's the one thing I can rely on in all of this." Ana realized that she missed him too. She suddenly felt bad for not saying it back.

CHAPTER 17

ONE MONTH LATER...

H is gut churned with worry. How would she feel about his plan? He valued her friendship, looked forward to seeing her. He hadn't been lying when he'd told her that he missed her. Missed her maybe a little too much maybe? There had been sense in Ash's words.

Would Ana hate him? Would she tell him to fuck right off? Part of him hoped that she would. Prayed that she would, but this was for the best. He had made up his mind, he was going to go through with it.

Deadbolts loosened and chains clanged. His heart sped up at the thought of seeing her, of holding her. He was so damned fucked. A key turned and the door finally opened. Her security gate was already unlocked. Ana was smiling, her face so radiant that it made his heart squeeze. She wore another one of those tight as fuck dresses. A dark blue one this time. It brought out the color of her eyes. Hugged her body like a second skin.

Her breasts were plump, her hips flared and yet she was tiny. Such an intoxicating combination.

Ana launched herself at him and he caught her. She wrapped her arms around him and he held on tight. "Two months is too long," she murmured as her hands threaded around his neck and covered his mouth with her own. Her tongue was hot and insistent. His dick sprang to life. Hard and throbbing in an instant. His balls felt like they landed in his throat. Ana moaned and pushed up against him.

Fucking hell!

He couldn't resist the urge to moan as well. He worked hard at not using his hands to explore her. Difficult when he could feel her hard nipples rub against him. When he could scent her arousal. *So damned sweet.* Her ass was mere inches away from his hands. He itched to touch and squeeze, to seek out her heat. It only bolstered the fact that he had indeed made the right decision. *No doubt about it!*

"Ana," he murmured against her mouth.

"Mmmmm," she half-moaned, half-replied.

"I was—" He chuckled as she tightened her arms around him, not ready to let him go yet. His zipper dug into his cock something fierce. "I was thinking…" He groaned when she pushed her chest a little more firmly against him. Seemingly oblivious to the effect it was having on him. A zing of need tightened his groin. "I was…" He peeled her off of him, putting her back on her feet. Her arms were still around him. "Thinking… we should go to the Dark Horse tonight." There. It was out.

Winston felt her stiffen. Ana pulled away, her expression serious. "Oh, okay… sure."

Fuck, this was hard. Way more difficult than he had

thought it would be. "It's just that I think you might be ready." She had asked him to tell her. It was the truth. Ana was ready.

"Ready?' She frowned, even giving a small shake of the head. "Ready for what?"

"We've fake dated lots of times now and you're doing really well."

She nodded. "Better than I ever thought possible."

"Exactly. As your friend, I declare you ready to take the next step like we talked about." He put his hands on her shoulders and squeezed. "You told me you might need pushing and well, I'm giving you the push you need."

"Do you really think so?" Her eyes widened, he could read fear in their depths.

He grabbed her hand. "I'll be there for you. I'll introduce you to one or two of the males. The good guys. The ones I would trust with my sister," he squeezed her hand, "if I had one."

"Your sister…" she nodded. "Okay. I'm not so sure it will work though." That same fear still wide in her eyes.

"I think it will. I think you're ready. Look at us… we're doing great. I've enjoyed texting back and forth," he chuckled. "There have been a couple of moments where I felt you were definitely ready."

She sighed. "If you really think so, then I guess…" Ana didn't look sure.

"I do." He nodded. They couldn't go on like this. Ash was right. He needed to do the right thing. The unselfish thing. "Unless you've changed your mind. Unless you don't want to—"

"I haven't changed my mind." She worried her lower lip for a second or two before squaring her shoulders. "I trust you, Winston, and if you feel I'm ready…" She mused for a while. He could see that her mind was racing a mile a minute. She looked away. "Well… thing is," she took a breath. "I know it's probably selfish of me but I would rather it be you than some…" Her eyes flicked in his direction before moving away again.

"No!" A growl. Much harsher than he intended. Ana flinched. He felt like an asshole. "It's not that I wouldn't want to. I think you're so incredibly beautiful, but…"

She rolled her eyes and exhaled. "It's fine. You don't have to explain. It was stupid of me to bring it up, I—"

"No." He shook his head. "It wasn't stupid. Far from it. We have chemistry, definitely more than friends should have but, thing is, I value our friendship too much. I would love to be the one to help you through this but I can't. We can't. Furthermore, I promised myself I would wait and I plan on sticking to that, unless of course you've changed your mind and are willing to think in terms of a relationship." He folded his arms.

"No!" Her eyes widened in horror. "I'm nowhere near ready for that."

"You see? I didn't think so. We're great as friends. We need to stick to that. I wish you would reconsider doing this though."

Ana pursed her lips. "You just said I was ready."

"You are."

Her eyes narrowed and her jaw tensed. "Then it's something I have to do. I'm glad you were honest with me." She sighed, looking him head-on. "I also value our friendship too much. You're right. Of course you are." She shook her head. "I'm sure you'll reach the top of that list soon and you'll find your Miss Right. And I'm sure I'll be dating… for real, by then, and everything will work out."

Despite their attraction, she really didn't see anything more there. Winston touched the side of her arm. "We've kind of done everything we can without totally crossing the friendship line. I think it's time." He held his breath, hoping that she would change her mind about this whole thing.

Her eyes brightened up. "Okay. I think I can do this. I can definitely try."

"I *am* right, otherwise I wouldn't suggest it." He felt guilty. Half the reason he was suggesting it was because he so badly wanted to forget about their friendship, forget about the pact he had made to himself, and rut Ana. She meant too much to reduce what they had to sex though. He had to go through with this. It was time to let her go. It was that or fight for her and he had a feeling, if he did that, she would run as far and as fast as she could.

"Okay." She smiled, looking completely relaxed. It was fucking killing him.

"Okay." He tried to sound happy about it when the truth was, he wasn't sure he would allow another male to touch her. He grit his teeth. Ana was his friend. His friend, dammit. He needed to do what was best for her and that meant moving on. Taking the next step. She needed to do this and he needed to let her.

Her expression changed. Frown lines appeared on her forehead and her eyes clouded.

"What's wrong?"

"You'll stay with me though? You won't just dump me, will you?"

"Not a chance. I'll be right there." What the fuck was he saying? "At least until…" He widened his eyes.

Ana rolled her eyes and laughed. "Yeah, yeah, we

spoke about this remember?"

He made a noise of confirmation and held his chest, pretending to be relieved when the truth was he felt anything but.

"Are you sure about this?" she whispered into his ear. "I might be having second thoughts."

Winston didn't say anything for a few seconds. He clenched his jaw, his golden eyes hardening up. Then he sighed. "Kane is a good male. He'll take care of you."

Kane was a sweet guy. It helped that he was attractive as well. He was the definition of tall, dark and handsome. His hair looked almost black. His eyes were a dark brown, like chocolate. He smiled easily. She should be giddy with excitement but she wasn't. She was calm though. No signs of an attack. That was something.

"So…" Winston folded his arms. He looked tense. Seemed a bit off kilter to her. He smiled and even that seemed a bit forced. "Tell us about something interesting that happened at the hospital this month." He glanced in Kane's direction. "Ana is a nurse – a human healer."

"I'm not really a healer, I assist the healers but yes, of course we had a couple of unique cases come in."

"What kind of cases?" Kane looked interested. Winston leaned forward.

"A guy and his girlfriend came into the emergency room." She couldn't help but smile. The things people got up to. "The doctor-on-call examined him." She shook her head. "He had a ring stuck around his… you know what."

"A ring?" Kane frowned. "What kind of ring?"

She pointed at the gold band on her pinkie finger. The one her grandmother had given to her before she passed away. "A ring like this, only it was an engagement ring. He put it on there to surprise his girlfriend. He wanted to ask her to marry him. He thought it would be a fun thing to do, I guess."

Winston grinned. "Noooo," he said.

"Yes." She grinned back.

"The thing got stuck?" Winston's eyes were animated. She nodded.

Kane was still frowning. "Why the hell would he put a ring on his dick?"

"It was as a surprise. She got so excited that she grabbed his member and… well… you can guess what happened."

"How the hell did he get the thing on there in the first place?" Kane shook his head. He didn't look impressed.

"He became aroused." Winston laughed. "And the ring got stuck."

"Very stuck." She was speaking to Winston, since Kane didn't seem to find it funny. "The tissues became inflamed from being so badly squeezed, so by the time he got his little erection problem under control, it was too late, the ring was stuck."

"Little erection is right," Kane snorted. "He should never have gotten a ring on there to begin with."

"What happened? How did they get it off?" Winston asked.

"The doctor had to carefully cut the ring off."

"No!" Winston's eyes were wide. So beautiful. She had meant to ask him what color his wolf was. It didn't seem right to do so now. Maybe tomorrow. Would he want to see her tomorrow? Last time he was in town they had spent Sunday morning together as well.

Surely they would remain friends? Of course they

would. She felt a pang at the thought of things changing between them. Why couldn't he have agreed to be 'the guy'? She knew why, but that didn't make this any easier. Also, why had he brought up a relationship, like he wanted one with her? It was probably just to prove a point, and it had worked.

"Then what? Was he okay?" Winston kept his focus on her, his words bringing her back from her thoughts.

"Um…" She pulled herself out of her funk. "He's fine. He was discharged the same day." She gave a small laugh. "They got engaged at the hospital. With all the drama, she forgot to say 'yes' during the actual proposal. It was quite sweet in the end."

"Yes, that is sweet." Winston looked sad.

"That's dumb." Kane shook his head. "I don't get humans." He finally smiled. "It was a funny story though." He hooked an arm around her waist.

Her heart rate sped up. His touch felt strange, which was completely normal since she hardly knew the guy. *Breathe! Stay calm.* Okay, she was okay. *Flip!*

So far so good.

Winston looked at Kane's arm and frowned, it was as if he could sense her unease.

"Um, Kane," he said.

"Yeah?"

"Maybe a round of shots before we hit the road."

"Mmmm…" she said. "That sounds good." Her nerves were a bit frayed. They were a lot frayed. Was it normal that she didn't actually want this? That she wasn't excited for it? It's just nerves. That's all.

"Yeah, why not?" Kane winked at her as he brushed past her on his way to the bar.

"What's wrong?" Winston looked at her pointedly.

"What if — ?"

"No 'what ifs,' you'll be fine!" Winston looked completely relaxed about it. If he believed in her then she should believe in herself, even if this felt all wrong. Just a few months ago, this was exactly what she wanted, to have casual sex, but now… she wasn't so sure. She didn't want to have sex with anyone other than Winston, which was wrong on every level since he was her friend. He'd made that very clear. If there was any doubt before tonight, it was totally cleared up now. He was the one pushing her to do this – but that was because she had told him to. *Arghhhh!* When had this become so complicated?

Winston may be attracted to her but he saw her more as a friend or a sister. *A sister.* Those had been his words to her. Ultimately, that was fine because she didn't want to ruin what they had either. If he thought she could go through with this. He'd painstakingly dated her, desensitized her and now introduced her to a couple of guys. The least she could do was try to make a go of it.

"Okay then," she whispered. "I'm going to leave with him. Are you coming back with us to the hotel? I mean, you're staying there as well, aren't you?"

He nodded. "Yes, I'll be in the same hotel, the shifters own the place so you don't have to worry."

"I didn't know that they owned it."

"Well, now you do. I'll be close by if you need me but I'm sure you'll be just fine." He brushed some hair behind her ear. She wondered if he knew he'd even done it.

"Wish me luck." She sucked in a breath.

"A female like you doesn't need luck." He leaned forward, his eyes on her lips. Then he looked wistful and kissed her forehead instead of her mouth. Not leaving together was weird. Having Winston kiss her on the forehead was weird. Things felt a little upside down.

"I do need luck." She watched as Kane picked his way through the crowd. He smiled at her. The guy was sweet and cute.

Winston gave her a dirty look. "Believe in yourself."

Ana nodded just as Kane arrived. He handed each of them a shot. They clinked glasses and drank. The alcohol burned its way down her throat.

"Come, Ana, let's get out of here." Kane slid his arm around her again. She waited a few seconds.

Everything seemed fine. She had this. Ana nodded. "Okay." She glanced at Winston. "I'll see you tomorrow then?"

He looked away, his Adam's apple bobbed. "Nah! I'm heading back early. There are a couple of things I need to do." *Things? What things?* She wanted to ask him but pushed back the urge. She didn't believe him for a second. Why didn't he want to see her? That was weird!

Winston hooked his thumbs in his jeans. In that moment she was convinced he cared. For just a second she was sure he didn't want her to do this. Then he grinned. His beautiful eyes glinted. Winston winked. "Have fun! Maybe I'll catch you next time I'm in town."

Maybe.

What?

Why?

"Call me," she said, a hint of desperation in her voice.

"Things are kind of crazy back home. Take care of yourself." Winston turned and walked away. Just like that. He was breaking things off with her. Not that they had anything. Not really. But what they did have was important to her. One of the women at the bar tried to grab him as he walked by, but he stepped out of her reach, disappearing through the door. Her chest hurt, her eyes stung.

Her heart suddenly sped up a whole hell of a lot. She realized that up until now, she didn't think he would hand her over like this. What had she expected from him then? That he would step in and take this fake dating thing to the next level? That didn't feel right either. He had tried to play the relationship card and she'd shot him down. The fact of the matter was that she wasn't ready for a relationship, not with Winston, not with anyone. He didn't want casual so they were stuck. Two people in different places in their lives.

"Ana." Kane was looking down at her.

"Oh." She swallowed hard. "Sorry."

"Are you okay?" His eyes were soft, his touch was soft as well.

She nodded. "I'm fine. Perfect." Her voice sounded too chipper.

His dark eyes narrowed with concern. "Are you sure? Do you want to stay for another drink, talk a bit more?" He breathed out through his nose. "We don't have to go back to my place. I could drop you off. Don't misunderstand me," his arm tightened around her, "I would love for you to come back with me, but only if you feel comfortable doing so."

What a sweetheart. She sucked in a deep breath. Good thing she'd donned her big girl panties before coming out. Not really, it was a tiny pink thong. "Yes, I'm sure. Let's get out of here." She was afraid. Hugely afraid, but she was more afraid of going home alone right now. Of failing. She had to do this… she had to move on. Winston had gone to a lot of trouble and she couldn't let him down.

CHAPTER 18

Winston was just pacing back towards the bed when his phone vibrated. It was on the side table next to his bed. He grabbed the device and checked the caller ID. *Fuck!* It was Kane.

"Yeah?" A rough growl. His heart was pounding in his chest.

"It's the human."

Winston could hear heavy breathing in the background. It was elevated, feminine and so full of fear. His own throat closed. *Fuck!*

"Let me go," he heard Ana say, she sounded terrified. His fur bristled, his hackles went up and all at once. His teeth sharpened, as did his vision.

Winston pulled on a pair of jeans. There was a ripping noise as his nails tore into the denim. He wasn't sure how, but he managed to get one or two of the clasps done up without slicing off his dick in the process. He'd managed to convince himself to go through the motions when he got back to his room. To take a quick shower and to get into bed. That had lasted all of five seconds.

He'd been pacing for the last few minutes, his mind conjuring up what was most likely going on down the hall. He was having to use every ounce of strength he possessed not to go and tear down Kane's door. One more minute and he would have. The fucking crazy thing was that he was happy the call had come in. Thrilled that Ana hadn't been able to go through with it.

Then he was plowing through the door and heading for Kane's room in a flat-out run. A hinge ripped as he tore into the male's room.

Ana was crumpled on the floor. Her eyes were wide, her skin pale. Still fully clothed. She was breathing hard, her arms wrapped around herself.

Kane was pacing. He stopped and turned. "Thank fuck! I didn't know—"

"What the fuck did you do to her?" Winston punched the male square in the face. Kane staggered back. His nose leaked blood but it wasn't broken. Deep down, Winston knew the male was not to blame for this. Problem was, Winston was freaking out.

"I didn't do anything." Kane put his hands up. "I tried to kiss her, that's it… I swear. I tried to kiss her and she started breathing funny. She tried to leave but I didn't think it was safe for her to do so. You told me to call you if anything went wrong. I didn't know what you meant at the time, but—"

"I… need…" Ana was breathing too quickly, "to… go…" Ana tried to stand up. She moaned, "Dizzy."

"I'm sorry, I—" Kane grabbed his head in his hands, he looked beside himself. "I'm so damned sorry. I don't know what's wrong. I didn't touch her, nothing happened."

"It's not your fault," Winston rumbled as he picked

Ana up. "I've got you." He worked hard at keeping his voice even. He needed to calm the fuck down so that he could get her to calm down.

"Dizzy… Winston… I'm…" She was panting hard. "I need to… need… I'm scared…" she sobbed, tears streaked down her cheeks.

"I have you now. You're safe." He cradled her to him.

"I didn't do a fucking thing, I—" Kane insisted.

"I know," Winston said. "It's my fault," he added as he left the room. Winston headed for his own suite, he had done research. He needed to calm her down, to get her breathing under control.

Winston kicked the door shut behind them after they entered the room. He sat on the edge of the bed holding Ana in his arms. "You're safe. You're with me."

Ana's eyes were wide. Her chest rose and fell in quick succession.

"Look at me."

Ana seemed to ignore him. "Home. Take… me… must go."

He clasped her chin in his hand. "Look at me, sweetheart," he spoke softly. "It's me, Winston."

She smiled even though she was still crying. Her breathing improved a bit.

"That's it. You're safe." He trailed the pad of his thumb down the side of her jaw.

"I couldn't do it." It fucking killed him to hear how sad she sounded. "I messed up."

"No, you didn't."

"I wasn't ready," a sob. "I knew it back at the bar. I should have listened to my instincts."

"It doesn't matter." He felt like the biggest dick alive for being happy that it hadn't worked out.

"I'm never going to be ready." Fresh tears streaked down her cheeks. He was happy to see that her breathing was pretty much normal, her color had returned as well.

"Yes, you will be," he spoke gently, caressing his hands down her back.

"All I want is to be normal. I want love. I want a relationship… long-term, I mean – but I can't even get this right."

"You are normal," he tried again.

"I can't spend the night with someone." She wiped away the tears, looking angry. "I'm so sick and tired of this. I just wish I could—"

"Shhhh." He kissed her mouth… her beautiful lips. Ana sighed against him. "Here," he said as he pulled away. Winston eased them further onto the bed, pulling the covers over them. "You're staying with me tonight."

"No," she shook her head, "I can't."

Winston frowned. "Are you feeling lightheaded again? Are you about to have another anxiety attack?"

"No." She shook her head some more and gave a very sad looking smile. "I'm with you, so I'm fine."

"Good." Winston laid down, he pulled her more firmly into the crook of his arm.

"You don't have to do this though." She lifted her head. Ana sniffed, her eyes filling with tears all over again. "I'm in your way. You don't have to feel obligated to have me stay over." She gave a snort, which was halfway to a laugh and halfway to a sob.

"Obligated?" He gripped the back of her head and looked her deep in the eyes. "That's where you have it all wrong. So very fucking wrong. I would be honored to have you share my bed… unless you want me to take the couch. I could—"

"Don't you dare." She shook her head, a smile played with the corners of her lush mouth. Ana snuggled into his chest. They were both still clothed. He in his jeans and she in her dress.

Ana sighed. He could almost hear her brain working.

"What is it?" he whispered, kissing the top of her head.

"I really hope I'll be able to have an orgasm with another person again one day," she said it jokingly but he could hear her underlying sadness, the very real fear.

Winston stiffened. Every part of him stiffened, especially one part in particular. What he wouldn't give to have Ana. To own every part of her.

This amazing female really believed that she couldn't do it. He knew for a fact and with absolute certainty that she could. He rubbed his hands up and down her back, feeling her relax. He was an asshole because his dick sprang fully to life. Her breathing eased and she pressed herself more firmly against him. He continued to stoke her back in long, easy strokes. Her breathing accelerated but not out of fear. Fuck, he caught a whiff of arousal. Ana didn't realize it but she was probably reacting to him. The female was more receptive than she realized. She made a soft moaning noise when he massaged her back a little deeper.

Fuck it! "Put your leg over my body."

"What? Why? Are you uncomfortable?" She didn't wait for an answer. "Like this?" She slid her thigh over his. The scent of her arousal increased a whole hell of a lot. He had to suppress a groan.

"I want to touch you a little." He put his hand on her thigh, rubbing up and down.

"Touch me?" Her voice was timid.

"Just a little." Her dress was already way up on her thighs. "Can I lift this a bit higher?" He touched the hem.

"Um…" Her heart was racing. Winston didn't scent fear though. He caught another snoutful of arousal. Fuck if his balls didn't take note. The suckers pulled right up. "Oh, I… You don't have to… you…"

"I want to touch you. Let me do this. I want to do this just as much as you need me to. You have to trust me on that."

"Okay… yeah…" Her breathing was definitely ragged but not in the same way as before.

Winston tucked the comforter more securely around her. He eased her dress up over her hips and pulled her thigh up even higher on his body, careful to avoid his raging hard-on. Didn't want to scare her.

"All you have to do is tell me to stop and I will." Her eyes were already hazy with lust. Her breathing was still elevated. Using one hand, he cupped the back of her head and closed his mouth over hers. The kiss was heated from the word go. It raged, consumed… it wasn't that he hadn't been with a female in a very long time, it was *her*. So fucking sweet. So full of passion.

Ana mewled into his mouth. She pushed herself against him. He could feel her plump, little breasts against his side.

He pushed a knee between her thighs and clasped a hand over her sex. Careful not to spook her. Her slip of a thong was soaking fucking wet. He bit back another groan. He rubbed her through the underwear a couple of times. Testing, giving her every chance to tell him to back off.

Ana moaned, her head falling back. She rocked against his hand. "Oh god! Oh, Winston." There was no sign of fear. Just pure, unadulterated lust.

He slipped one finger under the lace and zoned in on her swollen clit.

"Yes," a choked-out plea. His dick throbbed. It all out fucking throbbed. His balls hurt they were so tight.

He kissed her, swallowing her moans. When Winston slipped a finger into her tight as fuck pussy, it was his turn to groan. Her eyes flew wide open for a moment before squeezing shut. Her lashes fused. Her breathing turned ragged. He carefully thrust inside her, sure to zone in on that spot. So hot and wet. His thumb found her clit. Ana rocked her hips, she fucked his hand. He wished he could give her more, so much more. He wanted to give this female everything.

Her pussy was already fluttering around him. She was taking sharp little gasps of air. Her face was pinched. Normally he would drag out the pleasure, but she'd waited long enough. Winston added a second finger, keeping his thumb firmly on her clit.

Ana's back bowed as her body began to jerk against him. She bit down on her lower lip, her eyes wide.

"That's it," he growled. His voice was thick with a raging need. His teeth felt sharp. He wanted to bite her. To mark her. His cock twitched some more. Everything in him told him to put her on her knees and to take her… hard.

He ignored his own desires. A look of utter rapture took hold of her. Her mouth fell open. Her moans filled the room. Her hips still rocked against him. He slowed his thrusts, the pad of his finger eased the pressure on her clit. She mewled and gave a shudder as the last of her orgasm moved through her.

Ana licked her lips as she opened her eyes and

struggled to focus. Her cheeks were flushed. *Good!* She shut them again. He was loath to stop touching her. Winston grit his teeth. He eased his hand away from her and pulled her underwear back in place. Then he pulled her dress back down. Her breathing was normalizing. Ana smiled, she looked drunk. Her eyes were hooded. "Thank you," she whispered.

He stroked her head. "Sleep."

"No, really." She lifted her head, looking at him. Her eyelids were still heavily hooded. Her hair was mussed. In short, she'd never looked so fucking beautiful. His heart clenched painfully in his chest. "I appreciate it. I didn't think it was possible anymore. I—"

"No, it was *my* absolute pleasure. No need to thank me. It's no hardship touching you, I assure you. Ana, you are an amazing female."

She bit down on her lower lip, a cheeky glint appeared in her eyes. "I know we shouldn't but um… maybe…" her voice was husky. Her hand moved down his abs, she gripped him there, between his legs. He was fucked if his cock didn't do a happy dance.

Winston groaned. It took everything in him to take her hand and move it away. He squeezed. "No, as much as I would love to… take this further. We can't… we're friends, remember?"

He felt her tense against him. Her face went from relaxed afterglow to tense. "I don't understand. You just, we just—"

"We can't," he reiterated. "You know why. I made a decision and I need to stick to it." He tried to touch her but she moved back.

"You touched me out of pity then." Ana narrowed her eyes.

"That's not true. Not even fucking close. We're friends, I value you. I care more than you know." He reached out and this time she let him touch her. Winston cupped her cheek. "Please, I loved touching you."

"I loved you touching me?" She frowned. "Why then? Why can't we have sex? I don't understand." Her eyes clouded.

It hurt.

She didn't understand why exactly, but it did. Winston was right. Everything he said made perfect sense and yet it still hurt a whole hell of a lot. She'd gone from euphoria to down in the dirt, in seconds.

"We're friends, Ana." He ran a hand through his hair, sitting upright.

Friends.

Ana was sick of hearing him say that. Sick of saying it herself. She sat up and pulled her dress further down, suddenly feeling shy. It didn't matter that he made sense, she still wanted him. Burned for him. "We can still be friends if we… have sex."

Winston shook his head. His Adam's apple bobbed as he swallowed hard. "No, we can't." He pushed out a breath through his nose. "Truth is, I'm not sure we can be friends anymore, period."

At least he had finally said it out loud. She hated the way he'd implied it the whole evening. Her heart beat like a mad thing. The pain intensified. "Why not?" Her voice sounded distraught. She couldn't stand the thought of not having him in her life.

"My feelings for you…" He made a growling noise and gripped the back of his neck. "I don't see you as a friend anymore, Ana."

"What?" She frowned. "Why not? We are friends though, Winston, I love spending time with you. I look forward to it. You like me too, don't you?"

"I see you as more. I don't want to be just friends anymore. Tonight proved it to me. It almost fucking killed me to leave you with Kane. I was about to come and get you anyway."

Oh shit! Oh gosh! Oh no! She could feel her stomach clench and her eyes widen. This wasn't happening. Why had she pushed? Ana wasn't sure what she had expected but this wasn't it. "I can't," she blurted. "I told you I'm not ready for a relationship." As if on cue, her lungs seemed to close, her throat too. "Up until recently…" She struggled for air. "I couldn't even…" She gripped her throat. "Shit!" She may as well be on the moon, or deep in the ocean. That's how it felt right now.

An icy tendril of fear wound its way around her. She couldn't say that the fear was back. Fear never left her. Not really. It lived inside. Deep inside. Waiting. Waiting. Fear of death. Fear of living. Fear of others. Fear of being alone. Fear of allowing herself to want because to have was to lose. Fear of fear. Fear of this. Her throat closed some more. Sweat beaded on her forehead. The room closed in. Her clothes felt too tight but at the same time she was cold.

"Ana," his voice was filled with concern, Winston frowned deeply.

"Can't breathe!" She was panting heavily.

He gripped her forearms. "Look at me. Calm down."

"Can't!" she shrieked. "No!" she added, pulling away from him. She needed to go. Needed to… where was her purse? She looked about the room. Finally seeing it on the floor next to the door.

Thank god! She staggered off the bed and snagged the thin leather handle.

"No." Winston gripped her wrist. His hold was gentle but firm.

"Let me go." She tried to yank away but he wouldn't let her.

"I can't, Ana. Let me help you. What can I do?"

"Nothing!" she yelled between heavy breaths that didn't seem to contain any oxygen. Her throat closed some more. She was starting to feel light-headed. It wouldn't be long before she got dizzy and then she'd be stuck. She'd be too far gone to move. Once she was outside and alone she'd calm down.

"Please." His eyes were wide and filled with emotion. His grip tightened. "Let me help you."

"You can't!" she yelled. She just needed to be alone. The room tilted for a moment. She had to get out. Had to get away. "Need to leave." She was gasping. "Away from you."

"No, don't say that." His hand loosened.

"Let. Me. Go," she got out between ragged breaths.

Winston let her go so abruptly that she almost fell backwards. The room spun for a moment. They could talk in the morning. When things were more normal. She couldn't right now.

Ana turned and ran. She didn't look back. She couldn't.

CHAPTER 19

Winston followed Ana. His friend… who was he kidding? She had come to mean so much more to him. Infinitely more. He hadn't planned on telling her because there was sweet fuck-all he could do about it. Also because she didn't want him back. Sure, she wanted him to fuck her. Just like all the others, but he wasn't worth anything more. Just a fuck. A friendly fuck, which somehow made it worse.

He'd hoped that she wouldn't be able to go with Kane. That she'd realize that she had feelings for him. He'd been so fucking sure that she did. What an asshole he had been. Seeing her with Kane had only made his feelings deepen. His need for her had increased ten-fold. Maybe he had been wrong about Ana.

Winston watched as she leaned against a tree, her breathing eased after just a minute or two. Then she was digging in her purse and eventually typing on her phone. Ana leaned back against the tree. Her eyes were closed. She sniffed and wiped at her face. His chest tightened when he realized she was crying. Everything in him screamed to go to her, to comfort her but he knew deep down that his presence would have the opposite effect. *She doesn't want you or need you.*

Winston pulled himself further into the shadows. He hadn't planned on saying anything. Definitely hadn't planned on touching her. Feeling her tighten around his fingers. Hearing her surprised gasp as she tumbled over the edge. Seeing that look of rapture on her beautiful face had been everything to him. He shouldn't have blurted his feelings out like that. Should never have laid a finger on her. No, it was better this way. A clean fucking break.

Ana brought her phone up to her face, it became illuminated by the screen. She kept looking at it. Moments later, she made her way to the hotel parking lot. Her feet were bare. She hugged herself. His gut churned. It was safe within the hotel grounds but she wouldn't be safe once she left. Winston maintained a safe following distance.

Ana waved at the security guard in the parking lot. He waved back. "Are you okay?"

"I'm fine." She nodded. Her voice sounded fine. "Waiting for my cab. It should be here... there it is."

The guard smiled and nodded as the sedan pulled up to the curb. "Good to see you again."

"You too." Ana got in. Winston sprinted for his SUV as the cab pulled away. He followed the vehicle from a distance. Within five minutes, the cab pulled up in front of Ana's apartment. He watched her enter the building. It was only when the light came on in her apartment that he was able to breathe again. To relax.

Relax. Right. No! Relax was the wrong word. His gut churned. His hands clamped down even tighter on the wheel. He needed to distance himself from this female. Needed to stay the fuck away. It would be best for her. Best for both of them.

CHAPTER 20

"You look terrible," Edith said as she walked into her apartment. "And look at this place. Where is my friend? What have you done with her?"

"I decided to take a couple of days off, that's all." Ana sighed.

"Off of work or off of life?" Edith put her hands on her hips. "Because I can tell that you've done nothing other than eat take-out and let your dishes pile up."

"I'm all caught up on Netflix and I happen to like take-out."

"What's going on with you? You haven't returned my calls." Her friend narrowed her eyes. "You met up with Winston last weekend, didn't you? What happened? Did he hurt you, because if he did, I'm going to find—"

"No, no!" Ana put her hands up. "It's not like that."

"Something happened though."

Ana didn't answer. She wasn't sure she wanted to talk about it.

Edith held up a paper bag. "It's double chocolate. Get the spoons and start talking. I promise you'll feel better once it's out."

Ana nodded. "Okay."

Once they were comfortable, spoons in hand and a couple of mouthfuls down the hatch, she told her about the evening. All about going back with Kane and her panic attack. She skipped the part about the orgasm Winston gave her though.

"He rescued me and then told me he no longer sees me as a friend. He told me he has feelings for me."

Edith stopped, spoon halfway to her mouth. "What did you do?"

"What I always do... I panicked."

"And then?" Spoon still poised, eyes wide.

"I ran. I need to get away when I'm in the midst of a panic attack, it's the only thing that calms me down. I went back the next morning but he was gone." She sounded completely depressed. She felt completely depressed.

Edith finally ate the melting dessert. "Why did you go back? Had you changed your mind about starting a relationship with him?"

"No... I can't be in a relationship. I'm not ready." She shook her head.

Edith burst out laughing.

"What's so funny?"

"I hate to break it to you, hun, but you already were in a relationship. There was nothing fake about the two of you from the start. You *can* be in a relationship... you *were* in a relationship."

"Yes, as friends."

"Bullcrap. I told you that a man and a woman can't be friends if they're attracted to one another and I still stand by that."

"We were faking it." Even as she said it, she knew she wasn't being entirely true.

"Faking it, my ass. It was very real. The way you looked at him and the way he looked at you back. Friends don't look at each other like that. They certainly don't have heated kisses. Okay," Edith cocked her head, "you still haven't told me why you went back the next morning."

"I went to apologize." Ana looked down at the spoon in her hand. "I did a terrible thing. A selfish thing." She swallowed hard. "I asked for sex. I wanted to use him for my own pleasure. I ruined everything. Doctor Brenner was right, friends don't have sex with each other."

Edith laughed again. "Really now? You really believe that you were selfishly looking for a thrill. Did it never occur to you that you might have been looking for a way to get closer to him? To deepen your relationship? The fact that you're so cut up about it reiterates that you're in way over your head."

"No, I'm pretty sure I was looking for a cheap thrill. I let him touch me and… it was so darned good." Her whole body flushed at the memory.

"Touch you?" Edith's mouth dropped open. "As in… did you go to happy town?"

"I so did." She couldn't help but smile. "It made me want more. I'm selfish and terrible and a horrible friend."

"You're right, you are a horrible friend." Edith laughed when Ana widened her eyes. Edith must have seen the horrified look on her face because she quickly added, "Not to me." She sighed. "To Winston. You're a bad friend because the two of you *aren't* friends. You understand that don't you? It's not a bad thing that you want to have sex with him, he just needs you to own up to your feelings for him first."

"I'm not ready for all that." Ana grit her teeth, feeling frustrated.

"You are, hun, you so are. Have you ever stopped to think why you couldn't let that Kane guy get anywhere near you, yet you let Winston take you to happy town and even went so far as to want to have sex with him? You just need to get over yourself and admit to your feelings."

"Doctor Brenner says that I haven't given myself permission to move on. I want to so badly, but," a tear slid down her cheek, "I just don't know if I can. I think I've ruined things with Winston anyhow. He won't even read my texts, let alone reply to them. I've screwed up big time." More hot tears fell and she wiped at them.

"The guy is mad about you. Absolutely crazy. He'll come around. You need to have some patience. There's something else I need to ask."

Ana sucked in a deep breath. "I'm not sure I like the sound of that."

"Did you tell him what happened that night?"

"Sure, I may have left out some things, but he knows most of it."

"What things?" Edith asked, narrowing her eyes.

"Things I don't like talking about."

"You told him about John?"

Ana nodded. "Sort of. Not everything. I barely knew him when we spoke."

Edith's eyes narrowed some more. "Did you tell him about…?"

"I didn't tell him everything. I guess there's more he needs to know."

"I'd say." Edith shook her head. "Give him some

space. I'm sure he'll start responding to your texts."

"What if he doesn't?" She could hear the worry in her voice.

"Then go after him."

Ana nodded, she wiped her eyes. "I think I might just do that."

CHAPTER 21

ONE MONTH LATER...

Ana scanned the busy room. She clutched her drink to her chest as a couple pushed past. The cider was lukewarm by now, but she didn't care. She wasn't there to drink or to party. A group nearby broke out in laughter. The sound of music and insistent chatter filled the bar.

It was getting late. Too late. Soon people would start to leave. Most of them in pairs. The thought made her feel even lonelier. It was her own fault.

Where was he?

Where?

Maybe he hadn't come to Sweetwater this time. The thought made her heart clench. Made her eyes fill with tears. *No!* There was no way she was crying. She'd cried enough over the last month. The time had come for action.

"Hi, honey." A big man sidled up to her.

"I'm not interested." Her voice was flat.

"Leave her alone." The guy who had spoken was huge. He had dark hair and even darker eyes.

"Mind your own—"

The big shifter growled deeply. "Fuck off!" he snarled. The guy moved on.

The shifter approached her. He was frowning. "Are you okay?"

She felt her shoulders sag. A sigh left her. "No." She shook her head. "Have you seen Winston? Do you know him?"

The big guy shook his head. "He's not here. I'm not sure he even came through this time round. Look," the shifter looked at her pointedly, "I wouldn't worry about Winston. You do know that shifters rarely spend the night with a female more than once? You should not have developed feelings for him."

"It's not like that. He's my friend."

The guy grinned. "Yeah, right. You look lovesick. You scent lovesick. Winston is not on the list."

"I need to see him," Ana blurted. She had to see him. Had to speak to him.

The guy chuckled. "Not going to happen, female." He began to walk away.

"Wait." She gripped his elbow.

He turned. "What?" He licked his lips. "Want me to help you forget him?" It was weird because he didn't look in the least bit interested in her.

"No!" That came out a bit more harshly than she had intended. "I, um… have you seen Kane?"

The guy frowned. "Kane? Why the hell do you need to speak to Kane?" He folded his arms. "I thought you wanted Winston."

"No, there's nothing between Kane and me. I need to

ask him something, that's all." *What was this guy's problem?*

The shifter relaxed. "Oh, so you admit you have the hots for Winston?"

Ana rolled her eyes. "Yes, okay? I have the hots for Winston. I happen to be in love with him. Now, will you please tell me where Kane is?"

"You're too late, Kane already left."

<hr />

Ana was thankful that the guards at the hotel knew her. They knew of her friendship with Winston and had let her in, no problem. It gave her hope that Winston was there. She went straight to his room and knocked on the door. There was no answer. She tried a couple of more times before giving up. Then she went to the room that Kane had stayed in last time.

Her cheeks heated at the prospect of seeing the shifter. She was mortified. The guy had seen her in the throes of a really bad attack. He would think she was a looney tune and she couldn't blame him.

Ana sucked in a deep breath. It didn't matter. She needed to fix things. She knocked twice. There was no answer so she tried again. Just when she was about to leave, the door opened.

Ana tried not to stare. He held a shirt in front of his man-bits, otherwise he was completely naked. Come to think of it, he looked sweaty and his hair was mussed.

Kane grinned. "Hi… um… hi…" He'd forgotten her name. "Ana," he blurted, obviously suddenly remembering. Then he frowned. "Are you okay?"

"I'm fine. Sorry to bother you." His room was dark. Someone rustled the sheets of his bed. *Shit!* Just as she had suspected, Kane wasn't alone.

"No problem." He smiled.

"Kane." The woman in the room didn't sound very happy. "Tell her to go away."

Kane looked over his shoulder. "I'll be back in a minute." He locked eyes with her.

Ana had better make this quick. "Do you know where Winston is? I can't find him."

Kane frowned. "He didn't come with us this time. A couple of us tried to change his mind but he wouldn't budge."

Crap, she could feel her eyes fill with tears. Ana blinked hard a couple of times to try to keep herself from crying. "Oh." The word sounded choked. "Okay." She nodded, trying to swallow down the lump that had formed in her throat.

"I'm sorry, female. I know that the two of you are… close."

"Kane," a soft purr, "I'm getting lonely."

The big shifter rolled his eyes. "I need to go. Duty calls." He chuckled.

"Oh… of course. I'm sorry I bothered you. One last thing—" she quickly blurted before he could close the door.

"Yes?" He raised his brows.

"Please tell Winston that I need to speak to him. It's really important."

"Sure." Kane nodded. "I'll tell him. Good night."

"Good night," she said as the door closed.

CHAPTER 22

MONDAY AFTERNOON...

The bark was rough against his back. A cool breeze whistled through the trees. Birds chirped overhead. Winston rose back to his feet. He had rested for over an hour and yet he still felt tired. Sleep would have to wait. They needed to get back.

"Ready?" he asked. The other four males were in their furs, of course they were ready. The closest male gave a low growl.

He hefted the deer carcass onto his back and picked up a steady-paced jog in the direction of his village. Over logs, through brambles and over streams. On and on. His pack-mates padded next to him. It felt like he had run for hours. Finally, he scented smoke, he could hear the sounds of children playing. *Home sweet home.*

Within minutes, he entered the village, continuing until he reached the large kitchen. His four companions broke away, headed home. He circumvented the building and hoisted the deer onto a metal table outback.

Jackson stepped out onto the back step. "Wow!" he said as he laid eyes on the carcass. "That's one hell of a set of antlers, and enough meat to last for a couple of days."

"It was an older male, good meat but tough."

Jackson snorted. "I'll make jerky and stew. Tough meat is better than no meat."

"Absolutely." There had been no more run-ins with whatever had hurt Ward but hunting was becoming more and more difficult. Hunting parties had to travel farther and farther away.

Jackson looked worried. "I wish we knew what it was that was out there. Surely if they were an enemy they would have attacked by now."

"I don't understand it either," Winston agreed. "We need to maintain our vigilance."

Jackson nodded. "Anyhow, you go and clean up. I'm sure you can do with some rest."

Winston had been gone for over twenty-four hours. He'd asked for a hunt assignment. He'd specifically requested to haul the carcass. That way, he wouldn't have to speak to anyone. He hadn't been the best company of late. Winston wished he could head out on his own but safety in numbers was all important. He'd been especially cranky this weekend. Winston had volunteered to stay there, even though he missed Ana something fierce. He still believed it was for the best though. Ignoring her texts was becoming more and more difficult.

He nodded. "Yeah."

"Here." Jackson handed him a parcel. "Some food. I'm sure you're hungry."

"Starving. Thank you!" He took the parcel. Winston

could scent nuts, an apple, jerky and freshly baked bread. A thick steak would have been amazing but this would do the job just as well. It didn't help to complain.

Winston turned to leave.

"Oh," Jackson said, "I almost forgot, Kane was looking for you earlier. I think he's in the dining hall."

"Oh?" Why would Kane be looking for him? "Thanks." He walked around the building and into the large room. He spotted the male sitting with a group having lunch.

Kane looked up, he grinned, mouth full of food. Kane called him over with the sweep of a hand.

The male swallowed. "Hey," he said. "I ran into that sweet little human on the weekend."

Winston clenched his teeth. There was only one human Kane could be talking about.

"She came by the hotel, popped past my suite."

Motherfucker! Winston's hands curled into fists at his sides. "I don't want to hear about it," he growled, bile in his throat and already turning on his heel.

"No, bro! You have it wrong!" Kane yelled. "She was looking for you."

His heart beat a little slower, his blood cooled, just a little. "Me?" He turned back.

"Yes, she told me to tell you that she needs to see you. She has something important that she needs to tell you." He cocked a brow. "No idea what it was about." He shrugged and shook his head.

"Thanks!" Winston strode out of the dining area. Ana had been looking for him. *Why?* What could she possibly have to say? She probably wanted to tell him that she valued him as a friend. That she wanted to keep seeing him… as a fucking friend. *No, thank you!* He couldn't go down that road.

"Winston," someone called from behind him.

"Yeah?" He turned.

It was Ash. "I overheard your conversation with Kane." He smiled.

"Look," Winston put his hands up, "I don't plan on going to Sweetwater."

Ash folded his arms. "So," his smile turned feral, "I was right... there's something up with your female. She's the reason you've been acting like a bear with a sore head."

"I'm a wolf. I'm not a fucking bear." He smiled. It lasted all of a split second. "And my head's just fine. How many times do I need to tell you that she's not my female?"

Ash rolled his eyes. "If you say so. Are you in love with her?"

Winston squeezed his eyes shut. He couldn't help the deep sigh that was pulled from him.

"I'll take that as a *yes*."

Winston nodded. "Okay, but she doesn't feel the same way about me. Even if she did – and she doesn't – I'm not on the list so I can't act on it. I'm not going to fuck things up. I plan on obeying the lores."

"You done?" Ash raised his brows.

"Yeah."

"Your female was looking for you at the Dark Horse on Saturday night."

He frowned. "Ana went to the Dark Horse?"

"Yup." Ash nodded. "I kept my eyes on her and you'll be happy to know that she turned down any advances. I even made a move on her, but—"

"What the fuck, Ash?" Winston took a step towards

the male. His fur bristled beneath his skin.

Ash laughed. "I was just testing her. Calm the fuck down. I wouldn't do that to you. She turned me down flat, even told me that she has the hots for you."

"Ana said that?" Something eased in him. "Nah, that couldn't have been Ana." He shook his head.

"It was her. She asked about Kane and then went to the hotel so that she could give him the message you just heard."

"She said she has the hots for me?" *Could it be?* Then again, maybe it was all back to the sex.

"She did. Normally I wouldn't get involved, but you seem to really care for this female." He took a breath.

"I do. I care very much about her. I wish I knew why she went to the Dark Horse. Her real reason."

Ash narrowed his eyes. "She also mentioned that she was in love with you."

"What? Are you sure you heard her correctly?" Winston was too afraid to get excited.

"I'm a fucking shifter and an alpha... my hearing is just fine. That female is in deep. Just as deep as you are, by the looks of things," Ash chuckled. "I fucking told you so."

Winston could feel his heart pounding. The air seized in his lungs. "Fuck!" He ran a hand through his hair. "I can't believe it." He pushed out a breath. "Okay, good! Thank you for telling me. I won't fuck this up. I'll wait until the next Shifter Night to go and see her and we'll bide our time until my name comes up." He didn't try to hide his enthusiasm. "Anything is possible. Any-fucking-thing."

"Hold up!" Ash looked at him pointedly. "That female might be in love with you but you can't assume that she wants to mate you. It doesn't work that way with humans. This one is scared... I could scent it on her."

"You're right!" He could hear the disappointment in his voice. Humans could be strange creatures. Ana had been through a lot. "Shit!" He wished he knew what was going through her mind. Where she stood on this. How she really felt and why.

"Go," Ash barked.

It took a few moments for Winston to register what his friend had said. "Excuse me? What was that?"

"I said go. I already cleared it with Ward. You're useless to all of us like this."

"Go, as in...?"

"Go and talk with this female," Ash growled. "Sort out your shit."

Winston felt excitement rush through him. "To Sweetwater?"

"Yes, to Sweetwater, but you need to be back tomorrow."

"Thank you." He began jogging.

"Winston!" Ash barked.

He stopped and turned.

"I suggest you shower first when you get there. You're ripe, bro."

"I've been out hunting for the last few days. Give me a break."

"Have you seen how awful you look?" Ash gave him the once over. "Your chest is covered in gore, as is your back. Your hair is plastered to your scalp. Fuck, but you stink."

Winston grinned. "I'm excited to see Ana, but of course I'll shower first."

"And, you have to wait until your name comes up. No

exceptions. A little birdy told me that you don't have much longer to wait. Don't make assumptions though, she's a human."

Winston grinned. "My name is almost up?" His voice was animated.

Ash nodded. "Yeah. Go! I'll see you tomorrow."

That was all the urging Winston needed. "Okay, thank you! I won't assume anything." He took off in in a flat-out run, his fatigue forgotten. He was thankful Ash had urged him to clean up because he would've forgotten to do that as well.

CHAPTER 23

THAT EVENING...

Ana parked in her space, just in front of her apartment. It was late. She yawned and rubbed her eyes. Then she grabbed her purse and sucked in a deep breath. She hated this part. It was why she didn't work late shift much. Her whole body prickled as she got out of the car. She pushed the button to lock the car door and walked towards her building entrance. She had her cellphone in one hand and her keys in the other.

Her phone vibrated. She ignored it and kept walking. Her phone vibrated a second time as she reached the door to the building. Ana glanced at the screen.

Don't freak out!

It was from Winston; why would Winston send her a message like this? Then she scrolled down and almost dropped her phone.

I'm behind you.

"Winston?" she whispered.

"Yes," his deep voice punctured the dark. Then he

was behind her. Right behind her. So close she could feel his warmth. "It's me. You're safe."

Ana turned and there he was. Tall, oh so very tall. She had to crane her neck to look him in his eyes. His beautiful golden-brown eyes. She'd missed those eyes. She'd missed him so much. She wasn't sure whether she grabbed him or whether it was he who grabbed her. It might have been both of them at the same time. Next thing she knew, she was wrapped up in his arms though, in the tightest hug, and holding on like she never wanted to let go. A sob escaped. "It's you."

"I've got you," his voice was husky with emotion.

"I'm so sorry!" She could feel her eyes tearing up.

"I'm sorry too. I could've handled things better, I—"

"No, I had another one of those stupid attacks. I said things I regret. I didn't mean it…"

"Let's go inside." He pulled back, looking her in the eyes. "We need to talk this out. I'll understand if you panic but you need to understand that I'm not leaving. I'll stick it out with you. We'll do this together."

Warmth flooded her. "Okay… it's a deal."

She unlocked the door and they made their way up the stairs and along the hallway. Ana unlocked the security gate and the door and they went inside. She felt safe enough to forgo the deadbolts and the chain and merely pulled the door closed. She was safe with Winston. No one would dare break in or try anything as long as he was there.

"Would you like something to drink?" she asked, walking towards the kitchen. Winston followed. "Something to eat maybe? I'm sure you must be quite thirsty," she was babbling but couldn't stop. "You've come a long way. So, what have you—"

Winston gripped her hand and squeezed. "I don't want anything but you."

Wow! Direct and straight to the point. *Don't panic, Ana.*

"You know my feelings," Winston went on. "I'm in love with you and it's as simple as that. You're my Miss Right. The only female I want to be with."

She squeezed her eyes shut. Her breathing was definitely speeding up and she felt hot all over. "This is moving a bit quick. I'm not sure I can deal with…" She sucked in a few lungfuls of air. Those feelings of guilt returned. "I was so sure I could handle this but now that you're here… damn, it's hard." She looked down at the floor, working hard at staying calm. "Sex? I think so…" She looked him in the eyes. "Friendship – is a definite yes. Working towards more… I can do that too. The thought of a relationship scares me to death though." She shook her head, feeling lost. Feeling her skin tighten. "I don't know if I can go there."

"What are you saying?" He narrowed his eyes. "We were so connected the last time that we were together, that we almost had sex. We were this close." He held two fingers millimeters apart.

"That was fake. Completely fake. We were fake dating." She squeezed her eyes closed. What was wrong with her? Why had she said that? It was utter nonsense.

"It wasn't fake to me." His voice was deep, his eyes intense and locked with hers. He looked angry and hurt.

She pushed out a breath. "It wasn't fake to me either. I don't know why I even said that." Flip, she could feel the air thin. Ana gulped in a couple of deep breaths. "I need some water. I might need a few minutes to catch my breath."

"Take all the time you need." He stayed in the

doorway to the kitchen, giving her space. He leaned against the jamb.

Ana grabbed a water, she continued to breathe rhythmically. *Do. Not. Panic.* She could do this. "Do you want one?"

He shook his head.

"Okay, then." She took a deep drink, beginning to feel a bit better. "There's something important I need to tell you. I wasn't completely honest with you before." *Shit!* Edith was right. She needed to come clean before she could move forward.

He didn't say anything. Just stood there calmly, watching and waiting. There, but without pushing her.

"John was my husband." There, it was out.

Winston frowned. "You were mated? John?" He shook his head. "Your date? The male who was killed?"

She licked her lips and sniffed, trying hard not to cry.

"I'm sorry!" Winston walked to her and put his arms around her. "I'm so damned sorry. No wonder."

"We were married for three years. We were out celebrating…"

Winston nodded, his eyes firmly on her.

"Um…" Her throat tightened and a tear slipped out. "This is hard," she sniffed.

Winston pulled her into a tight hug. "Take your time." His voice was thick with emotion. "All the time you need."

Several minutes passed. "I didn't tell you because I hate to talk about it." She paused, another long minute passed. "We were celebrating because…" She bit down on her lower lip for a moment, trying to compose herself. "I was pregnant," she finally blurted, her voice muffled against his chest. *Thank god that was out too!* Winston tried to pull away, so that he could look at her, but she held tight. "No, don't! I had just found out that I was having a boy... we were going to have a little boy." She made a sobbing noise, breathing deeply to try to keep control. "We were so excited. John decided to take me out to celebrate." She turned her face into him and sobbed. It still hurt. Four years later and she could still remember it like it happened yesterday. "After it happened, after John was killed and they took his body away, I started having cramps. They rushed me to the hospital. They did everything they could." She was still crying, her breath coming in gasps.

"Oh, Ana..." Winston held her, he rubbed his hands up and down her back. "I'm so sorry." He held her tight.

"I lost them both that night. My husband and my baby. My family... my whole world."

"I'm so fucking sorry," his voice was choked.

It took a few minutes to compose herself. She pulled away, using her hand to wipe at her face. "I don't understand why he didn't listen." She wasn't sure where that had come from, or the anger. This was new.

Winston was frowning deeply.

"Why didn't John just hand the stuff over? They were things. Stupid, replaceable items." The anger inside of her grew and grew. "The guy was a two-bit criminal!" She was shouting now. "He was more afraid than we were. The gun went off. If John had just cooperated. If only he had listened – he'd still be here. We would have our baby." The pain was back, it blossomed inside of her. "Why didn't he just hand it over? Why did he have to fight? Why?"

"He did it because he loved you. He loved both of you." Winston clenched his jaw, his eyes were tormented. "He was trying to protect his female and his unborn child."

She was crying again. Enough with these damned tears. "John loved me very much. We'd been trying for over a year for a baby. So, maybe you're right." Ana realized how much better she felt. She'd never realized how angry she was. How much she had blamed John for her being alone. For what had happened. "I've been holding onto all this anger. I didn't even realize."

"It sounds like he was a good male."

"He was." She smiled. "He was a good partner."

"I would have done the same, in a heartbeat – if you were mine. I agree with him on that. I understand if you need time, if you—"

"I need you, Winston. I'm completely and utterly in love with you. Edith and I talked about it but I didn't realize it until one of your shifter friends brought it up," she waved a hand, "at the Dark Horse. I was looking for you, I… it isn't important."

"That was Ash. My best friend, he was the one you mentioned it to."

"Did he tell you?"

Winston nodded.

"So you knew," she gasped. "Why didn't you say anything?"

Winston nodded. "Yeah I knew, but I needed to hear it from you." He stepped in closer to her, cupped her face in his warm, calloused hands. "I love you so damned much."

"I'm so sorry. I should never have asked you for sex. It wasn't because I wanted to use you. I guess I wanted to be closer to you but I didn't know how."

"I understand. I was upset, I'll admit it, but I

understand better now."

"Does that mean we get to have sex now? I might just be able to this time…" Her eyes widened. "I hope." She looked upwards. "I pray. Can we at least try?"

"No." He shook his head.

"No?" Her voice was laced with frustration.

Winston chuckled. It was a warm, rich sound. "It could be months before I make the list. It might even be as long as a year. Ash told me it's coming up, but it could still take time. I'll only be able to see you on Shifter Nights. With all the shit going on, it might not even be that often." He turned really serious, frown lines marred his brow. "It wouldn't be fair to make you wait like that."

Ana laughed. She rolled her eyes as well for good measure. "A few months? I've waited years… you might still have to wait until I'm forty-nine before…" She wagged her eyebrows. "Before we can have sex."

Winston kissed her softly. "We'll have to take things really slow then," he said as he pulled back.

"Not too slow though. I'd like to try that orgasm thing again."

"Oh, I would fucking love to make you come. I'm going to pick you up now."

She nodded. "Okay."

He lifted her off of the ground and kissed her. Then he pulled back. "Would you prefer the sofa or your bed?"

They'd hung out, as friends, on her sofa. "Bedroom," she whispered, threading her hands around his neck. It was time to step this up.

Winston growled low. He carried her to her bedroom and gently put her down. She lay back. Just like before, Winston pulled the comforter over them. "Light on or off?" He kissed her neck.

Ana moaned softly, feeling his teeth rake over her flesh. "Don't care," she blurted. Her breasts felt heavy, her clit throbbed. She knew she was wet.

Winston kissed her until her mind short-circuited. Until her toes curled and her pussy clenched with need.

Winston stroked her through her jeans. *Oh god!* She moaned. It felt good but it wasn't nearly enough. She jerked her hips against his hand. It was like they had a life of their own. Then her pants were undone and his fingers were there. She moaned so loudly that her throat hurt. The pad of his finger zoned in on her clit. Her back bowed. Her skin felt tight. She parted her legs as wide as they would go with the stupid jeans in the way. That coiling sensation had already started. She couldn't catch her breath, but in a good way.

There was a tugging on her jeans as he eased them down her thighs. Then he was raking his teeth over her nipples, right through her sweater. He circled her clit with his finger and she cried out, her hips bucking.

There was a hard shove and her jeans came off one of her legs. "I'm going to put my mouth on you now." Winston was under the comforter. "Stay calm. Let me know if you feel uncomfortable."

She had to stop herself from pushing him down where she needed him – and where she needed him was there… right there… right… there. She gave a yell as his hot mouth closed over her nub. Her very sensitive, very needy nub. Winston suckled her for a few seconds before laving her with his tongue. When he sucked her again, he pushed two fingers into her as well. Her skin was so tight that she was sure it was going to split. She was burning up. Tighter, tighter, higher, higher… almost…

She gave another hard cry. Her breathing had been

reduced to hard, sharp pants.

Winston stopped and lifted the cover. "Are you okay?"

"No!" she practically shouted.

"What can I do? How can I—"

"More," she panted. "Please, Winston."

His eyes widened when he realized that she was fine. Then he grinned. So sexy, so incredibly gorgeous. "No problem," he murmured. He thrust two fingers into her. His mouth sealed over her clit and she was tickets.

Ana shouted out as everything let go. Pleasure rushed through her. She closed her eyes, her head falling back. She gripped the covers so hard that she was sure she heard a nail crack. Her hips rocked against him.

She finally fell back on the pillows. Winston laved her clit softly as she came down. Ana struggled to catch her breath.

"Are you okay?"

"No, I'm not." She shook her head wildly from side to side.

He frowned, getting off of her. "What can I do?"

Ana pulled her sweater over her head. Then her shirt. She unclasped her bra. Winston kept his eyes on hers, which was commendable. He swallowed thickly. "We don't have to do this. We can wait."

"I don't want to wait. I want you and you want me. I need this. I need you, Winston."

"We said we would take it slow." He looked really worried. It warmed her that he cared so deeply for her.

"We will. We are. We fake dated until we weren't faking. Now we can date for real… that means sex… lots of sex when you're here once a month. By the time you're on that list we'll be ready to—"

"To make you my Mrs Right," he said when she let the sentence die.

"I might still struggle a bit at times. It might not all be smooth sailing, but I love you. I want you."

"You're sure?" He swallowed again.

"So very, very sure, you have no idea."

"Really?"

"Yes, really but only if you're sure too?"

He finally looked down at her breasts. Winston groaned. "I've never been more sure in my entire fucking life." He cupped them in big hands. "So soft and perfect."

He leaned forward and kissed her softly. When he pulled back, his eyes were glowing a little. It was beautiful. He was beautiful. "I'm too far gone here." He gripped her hips, his hold firm, even a little rough. "It's been so long and I want you so damned much."

"I'm on the pill," she whispered. "I want you too. Just take me. I'm wet and ready."

Winston groaned again, deeper and louder this time. His grip tightened for a second and then she was on her knees. He'd flipped her over like she weighed nothing. Winston caged her with his body.

She waited for the panic to set in but it didn't happen. She felt safe and loved with this shifter. This felt right. "Is this okay?"

"Yes," her voice was thick with need.

"I've had several wet dreams, all involving you, on your knees."

"Oh, yes."

"Yes," he growled the word. "You are so damned beautiful. Better than I imagined." He palmed her ass with one hand. She heard a zipper go down, felt his thick, heavy cock hit her ass cheek. "You tell me if you can't take it. If you need me to stop. I can wait… as long as it takes." His voice was thick and husky. "Tell me."

A shiver raced up her spine. "Yes?"

"Did you use that dildo like I told you to?"

She broke out in goosebumps. "I did."

"Good. I'll take it slow."

"I want you." She could hear the certainty in her voice. He must have too because next thing his cock was there. Right there where she needed him.

He rubbed on her clit in lazy circles with his finger, the head of his cock put pressure on her entrance but he didn't actually breach her. It was like he was testing. Checking.

So sweet.

Ana whimpered. He rubbed her clit a little quicker, using a bit more pressure. "Yes!" She was thrusting her hips, pushing backwards. She leaned down so that her breasts were rubbing against the comforter. Even that felt good. All of her senses seemed heightened.

Winston groaned as he pushed into her. It was his turn to sound out of breath. "Fuck!" he growled. "So good!" he added on another moan. "I need to rut you… hard… please don't be afraid." She could feel him shudder.

Excitement coursed through her at the prospect of him doing just that. Then she realized that he was waiting for her confirmation. "Yes," she sobbed.

He pushed the rest of the way in with a hard thrust.

Ana shouted his name as his balls hit against her. It stung a bit. She'd never been so stretched. So full. Her headboard knocked up against the wall on the next thrust. It hit again and again.

Her throat hurt from all the cries. His finger kept up its soft rub, rub against her clit. It was like she was going out of her mind. It amazed her how he could fuck her so hard and yet touch her so softly at the same time, almost with reverence.

Suddenly, Winston stopped, mid-thrust. He was shaking from head to toe. "Are you okay?" His voice was deep with need.

"I'm fine." She swallowed thickly. "I'm good." She was panting hard. "I want more," she managed to grind out.

The words were barely out and he was thrusting again. The headboard had to be knocking a hole in the wall. Not that she cared. Ana gripped the comforter. She could feel her pussy flutter with the start of her orgasm. If he stopped now, she would die. Her heart would quite literally give in.

"I'm good!" she shrieked. "Oh god… I'm so good!" she yelled. "I'm awesome! Awesome!" She screamed as her pussy began to spasm. She screamed his name as her orgasm took her.

Winston jerked against her, his fingers digging into her hips. He growled low and deep, sounding like a ferocious animal. The sound excited her.

Winston slowed his movements, until he finally stopped. He was breathing hard.

So was she, but in a good way. In the best way. Ana found that she was grinning so hard that her face hurt. "That was amazing. So good."

He carefully pulled out of her and took her into his arms. Winston kissed her long and deep. "I love you so much," he said as he released her; he was grinning as well.

"You fixed me." Her voice was filled with awe.

"You talk such shit." He swept the hair from her face.

"There was nothing to fix. You were perfect to begin with." He kissed the tip of her nose before rolling on top of her.

"We can't cuddle."

"Why not?" Her voice was husky.

"Because you can still talk."

She frowned. "Yeah and… that's a bad thing?"

"Very bad. You shouldn't be able to talk or walk."

He spun her around so that Ana was on top. She squealed. "This has been another fantasy of mine."

"I've had a few of my own," she said, looking at him through her lashes. Her lips were swollen. Her breasts were amazing. Perfect mouthfuls he planned on sampling every chance he could get.

"Have you now?" He raised his brows.

Ana nodded. "I thought of you every time I used that dildo." She slid forward so that her pussy was flush with his dick.

He groaned, feeling how wet she was.

"You'll have to show me sometime," he rumbled. "Right now, I want you on my cock."

Her pupils dilated. Ana lifted and he positioned himself at her entrance. She slowly dropped onto his length. So fucking tight, it almost blew his mind.

Then she began to move. Slipping and sliding all over his dick. Up and down. Her eyes were glassy with lust. Her little breasts bounced.

Winston gripped her hips and fucked her from below. He angled his hips until she cried out. *There!* Then he licked his thumb and gently rubbed on her clit.

Ana's head fell back and she gasped. She was moaning with every thrust. He could feel that she was close so he eased off of her clit. He wanted to draw out her pleasure.

"So good," she ground out. "Oh god."

She was a vision. Her hair loose. Her cheeks flushed. Her eyes glassy with pleasure. Her nipples tight. Winston sucked his finger and moved to a sitting position, scooting to the headboard. He widened his legs a tad, continuing to thrust. It didn't take him long to find that spot. Her moans became louder. Her breathing ragged. Her breasts rubbed his chest. Hard and soft.

Her eyes were wide.

"You trust me?"

She nodded. "Yes." A moan.

"Good." He pushed the tip of his finger into her ass and she went off like a rocket.

Ana shouted his name, squeezing the fuck out of him. Two thrusts later and he was coming too. He grit his teeth, which had partially erupted. He needed to keep his canines far away from her during sex. All he wanted was to mark her. Take her. To make her his. Soon. Very fucking soon.

Winston growled low as he came, pulling her close. Ana called his name a second time, whispering it a third as she fell against him. He cradled her in his arms.

"I thought you were full of shit," she slurred her words. "About the whole butt thing," she added, still trying to catch her breath. She giggled, sounding out of breath.

"Oh that." He chuckled, slipping out his finger. "That was nothing. Just wait until I bite you."

She shivered in his arms.

Winston rolled her over and hoisted her legs onto his shoulders.

"Again?" She gave him the sweetest smile. Her eyes were hazy. "You can't be serious."

He began to move and she moaned. "Oh yeah, I take fucking very seriously."

She tensed up. "I thought you were done fucking."

"Meaningless fucking. I'm only just getting started on you though."

"Oh good, but… I don't think I can." She moaned again.

"Oh yes, you can." He found her clit.

Ana groaned, low and deep. "Maybe."

"Definitely." But Ana was moaning too loudly to answer him.

CHAPTER 24

~~~

THREE MONTHS LATER...

Ana took another pile of shirts and placed them in her suitcase. She moved back to the closet and picked up the pile of jeans next.

"I can't believe you're leaving," Edith sighed. "How long have we been friends for?"

"Since we were seniors in high school."

"Exactly. That's a long time." Edith looked wistful. She stretched out on Ana's bed, propped herself up on the headboard and pulled a pillow into her arms. Hugging the pillow, she sighed again. "I'm going to miss you so much." She tossed the pillow to the side and scrambled up into a sitting position. "Don't get me wrong, I'm so happy for you. Crazy happy. I'm also a little jealous though."

"You shouldn't be." Ana shook her head, leaving the jeans where they were. "There's a guy out there for you." She sat down on the bed next to Edith.

"Guy shmuy!" Edith pulled a face. "I've pretty much

given up on my search for love. That's not it, I'm jealous of Winston."

Ana widened her eyes. "I didn't realize you harbored a secret crush on me." She laughed.

Edith joined in. "No, you idiot," her friend finally said. "I'm going to miss this. How we lean on one another. Our ice-cream nights. They won't be the same, in fact, I'm going to lose weight. One thing to look forward to."

"You look fantastic, my friend. You don't need to lose any weight. Not a single pound." Ana took Edith's hand and squeezed. "Leaving is the one really shitty thing I have to do if I want to be with the man I love. Leaving my family, my friends and you." She squeezed her hand again.

"I see I got my own category." Edith's eyes glinted, then she frowned. "It was separate from the friend category, which worries me." She cocked her head, looking serious. Ana noticed that the glint was still there though.

"That's because you're not just a friend, you're my very best friend and that deserves a category all of its own."

Edith's eyes grew misty, they welled with tears.

"I'm going to miss you too," Ana said as they wrapped their arms around one another. "So very much. I wish I could pack you in a suitcase and take you with me."

"Me too," Edith murmured as they released one another.

"I'll visit often." Her voice was soft, still thick with emotion.

Her friend rolled her eyes. "Yeah right."

"Every month or so." Ana smiled. "I hope you'll come

to the wedding? The shifters call it a mating ceremony."

Edith's eyes lit up. "You mean I can visit you?"

Ana nodded. "My closest family is allowed to visit on special occasions."

Edith frowned. "But I'm not family."

"You're my very best friend, and that makes you family in my book. You're coming to the wedding – if you want to that is?"

"Of course I do. You don't even have to ask. I'll take a few days leave. It'll be amazing."

"I'm pretty sure you won't have to wait too long after that to come through again." Ana could hear the excitement in her voice.

"What do you mean?"

"Just that there might be plenty of special occasions in my future." Ana couldn't help but smile. "We plan on trying for a family quite soon after we are mated and—"

Edith squealed. "Seriously? Oh, my gosh! Aren't you guys rushing into things?"

Ana shook her head. "Nah, we don't think so. We have to live together for three months before we can mate. The shifters give the time period to make sure that we humans enjoy living out in the middle of nowhere, that we're serious about mating. Shifters mate for life."

"A cooling off period."

"Cooling off… I think the opposite will be true." Ana bobbed her brows. "I can't wait to see Winston every day… spend every night with him."

"So, no more panic attacks?" Edith asked.

Ana shook her head. "Nope! I've had moments of anxiety but nothing out of the ordinary. I'm happy to say that my days of having to breathe into brown paper bags and of puking on people are over. Doctor Brenner says it's admitting to my anger at John that did it. Winston has also had a big hand in it. Not pushing me... just being the sweetest boyfriend a girl could ask for." She paused, gathering her thoughts. "It was also letting it go. As well as finally giving myself permission to move on. I will never forget John or my baby." She put her hand on her belly. "I will always love them, but I'm still here." Her voice became soft. Her heart still gave a clench remembering the family she used to have. It wasn't unbearable anymore though. She would never forget either of them, but at least now she could turn to the future. She could think of all the amazing things in store for her, for both her and Winston.

"I'm so happy for you. I'm so glad you've been able to embrace your future."

"Your guy is out there somewhere," Ana said.

"Nah, I told you I've given up. I'm throwing in the towel. I'm done." Edith looked resolute.

Ana laughed. "You know what they say, right?"

She could see that Edith wanted to roll her eyes. She sighed instead, a smile toying with corners of her mouth. "Okay, tell me... what is it that *they* say?"

"You'll find your guy when you stop looking. Since you say you've stopped..." Ana shrugged.

Edith laughed. "Somehow I doubt that I'll magically find someone simply because I've quit looking."

"Just you wait and see, he's going to sweep you right off of your feet."

"I'd have to see it to believe it." Edith looked skeptical.

"One day we'll look back on this conversation and you'll tell me I was right."

Edith pulled a face, it was clear that she put no stock in it.

CHAPTER 25

———————— // ————————

T hey stood beneath a large oak tree. The wind gently caressed Ana's hair. She bit down on her bottom lip. Winston pushed the gold band onto his soon-to-be mate's finger. It slid into place next to the diamond solitaire. The shifters had adapted their mating ceremony to include some human traditions. Ana smiled through her tears, which sparkled on her lashes in the afternoon sun.

"You okay?" he whispered.

"So happy." Her smile widened and his heart almost fucking burst from sheer love for this female. She wore one of those poofy white gowns adorned with sparkling crystals and pearls. Her breasts looked superb in the corset top. Her hair was piled high on her head, her ears sparkled with diamond earrings. She was a vision. So beautiful, she threatened to steal his breath. He was the luckiest male alive.

"I wish you both a long and happy life together," the

elder went on. "Many moons. May your home be filled with happiness, laughter and may you be blessed with young ones." He continued, "I hereby declare the two of you almost mated. You may kiss your female."

Ana frowned. "Almost?"

Winston crushed his lips to hers. His female's hands threaded around his neck. He swallowed her gasp of surprise as his tongue breached her mouth. He wasn't fucking around here. Ana was his... finally... well, almost at any rate. He broke the kiss, looking deep into her eyes. "I love you," he whispered.

Not waiting for her response, he hoisted her over his shoulder. The humans in the crowd gasped. The shifters hollered and cat-called.

"Winston!" Ana's voice was laced with surprise and possibly a little embarrassment. "Put me down." She kept her voice low.

He began walking towards their home, taking big strides, careful not to jostle her too much.

"Winston!" she yelled.

"Where is he taking her?" Ana's mother asked, sounding worried.

"It's all a part of the ceremony," Ash said, he could tell that his friend was smiling. "They'll join us a bit later at the celebration."

Somewhere in the distance, Edith and Doctor Brenner laughed their asses off.

"Does he have to manhandle her like that?" Winston detected a hint of excitement in his mother-in-law's voice.

Ash chuckled, he said something back but Winston was too far away to hear what it was.

"What are you doing?" Ana was wriggling. "Put me

down."

Winston slapped her ass through all the layers of her dress. "I'm making you mine."

"What are you talking about?" He pushed the door open to their home and quickly made his way to the bedroom. "I *am* yours... Winston." She growled his name. The way she said it had his balls pulling tight.

"No, you're almost mine. Almost."

"Oh!" She gasped when she realized why they were here. "We're going to consummate our mating now. As in right now?" she gasped. "We can't. What about our guests?"

Winston allowed her to slide gently down his body. Her face was a little red from hanging upside down and her eyes were a bit dazed. "We should wait until after the —"

"I'm done waiting." He cupped her jaw. "I've waited long enough. Do you know how hard it's been to be buried deep inside and not sink my teeth into you?"

He watched the column of her neck move as she swallowed thickly. Ana shook her head.

"I've had to deny every instinct." He clenched his teeth. "I won't wait. I'm making you mine and then we can head to the ceremony."

"Okay." Her voice was breathy. "I love that you're this impatient."

He spun her around, there were what looked like a thousand little buttons all along the back of the corset part of the dress. He growled, his big hands felt clumsy when trying to undo one of them. The buttons were looped through a tiny thread. "This dress is..."

"Don't tear my dress." She glanced back at him as he unleashed a string of curses, all under his breath.

"Fine," he conceded, pulling the fabric down so that her breasts spilled out the top. "Much fucking better," he sighed taking one of the pink tips into his mouth. Come to think of it, she was gorgeous in the dress. Her little tits pushed up high over the lace. Ana was the perfect combination of sweet and sexy. She moaned when he sucked on a plump nipple. Groaned when he nipped on her flesh.

Then he grabbed her by the hips and placed her on the bed. "We'll work around the dress."

"Okay." Her voice had grown husky. A sign of how turned on she was.

He pushed up all ten layers of chiffon and lace. Okay, there probably weren't as many as ten layers, but it felt like it.

Her pussy was covered in a tiny scrap of white lace. He could see her thin strip of fur. His mouth watered. Ana opened her legs and arched her back. The fabric was soaked through. Using one finger, he traced her slit softly. Ana squirmed. Then he closed his mouth over her clit, sucking on her right through the fabric. She whimpered. Impatient now, he pushed the fabric aside, enjoying the view for a few seconds. Glistening flushed pink. Her clit was swollen. He laved the bundle of nerves using the tip of his tongue.

"Fuck," his sweet mate cursed loudly. Ana had completely come out of her shell over the last few months. "God, yes!" she yelled when he laved her again. "Suck it," she begged.

Winston held back a chuckle. He did as she asked. Ana's hips bucked as he closed his mouth over her clit. She gripped his hair, rocking against his mouth. "Oh yeah! Oh!" He inserted two fingers and pumped them in and out of her. Winston knew he should take it slow but he was too damned impatient. He had meant what he said, his patience was all but gone. His canines felt sharp against his tongue. He sucked, licked and continued to pump those fingers. Ten seconds later and she was flying apart with a hard yell.

"You are so good at that," she said, panting.

Winston smiled, his face felt taut and his dick all out fucking throbbed, as did his gums.

"It's why I mated you. You're fabulous in bed."

"Is that the only reason?" he asked.

Her eyes glinted and her mouth twitched. She shook her head. "And because you have a big cock." Her eyes dipped to what could only be a huge bulge in his suit pants.

"Really now?"

She nodded. "And because I love you so very, very much." Her eyes misted. "You're everything to me."

"Fuck!" he snarled, trying not to sound like an animal… and failed. "Sorry." He squeezed the back of his neck. "My instincts are riding me hard right now." He pulled on the lace covering her sex, it shredded apart. "I need to fuck you now… seriously fuck you. I need to make you mine, Ana." He looked from her pussy to her beautiful face.

She swallowed thickly and nodded. "I can't wait to be yours."

"I'm going to bite you."

"I know." A flash of fear crossed her face.

"It'll feel amazing, I promise."

"I trust you, my love."

"Good." Another low growl caused his chest to vibrate. "I'm sorry, I'm just so turned on. So desperate to mark you."

Ana reached up and cupped his jaw. "You don't ever need to apologize to me. I told you, I love your wolf. I love how beautiful your eyes look right now. So golden and glowing. I love how sharp your teeth look and how desperate you are for me. I feel the same way about you."

"Good." He reached down and unclasped his belt. His hand actually shook as he undid his pants. Instead of taking his cock out, he moved to his shirt and undid the buttons, loving how greedy Ana's eyes had become. Loving how she licked her lips as he pulled down his zipper. His dick sprang free. It was like the horny fucker was trying to get at her. Couldn't say he blamed it one bit.

"You ready?" he asked, his gaze raking over her body. Her beautiful little breasts spilling over the corset. Poofy dress bunched up around her hips. Glistening pussy and ripped lace between her thighs which were splayed for him. All for him.

Ana nodded. She threaded her hands around his neck and pulled him onto her.

"Wrap your legs around me." His voice was a rough rasp, tight with need. She did as he said, so hot and so wet. He couldn't fucking wait to push inside her. Face-to-face. Chest-to-chest. He wanted to watch her come. Wanted to feel her shake beneath him as he bit down into her.

Forcing himself to calm the fuck down, he kissed along the column of her neck. He sucked on her ear. Ana moaned. Then he took her mouth and kissed her. So good he could hardly breathe. He pulled back, watching her face contort in pleasure as he sank into her. Slowly. Oh so slowly.

Ana whispered his name. Balls deep. Her pussy so snug, so damned wet. "You feel amazing."

"So do you." She was panting.

He pulled her thighs high, sinking in deeper. Ana moaned. "Love you," he growled as he began to move. Hard, slow thrusts that had her shouting out from the word go. His balls were already tight. So close to coming it was scary.

Winston sucked on the tip of a finger and slid his hand between them, quickly zoning in on her clit. Her eyes widened and her groans became deeper. He kissed her and moved back to look at her, and then kissed her again. Loving how the pleasure enhanced her beauty. Eyes wide and glassy, cheeks flushed. Jaw tight as her little fingers dug into his back. Her heels did the same. Her yells grew louder, deeper. He sounded like a fucking beast. Grunting and groaning. His teeth felt huge. Thankfully, they didn't seem to scare her. The opposite seemed true.

Her gasps grew short and choppy. She tightened around him and then she was letting go. Her jaw turning slack as her pussy clamped the hell out of him.

Winston ground out her name as his own orgasm hit. *Careful! Easy! Take it slow!* He leaned in as she was coming down. *Softly!* Using every ounce of willpower he possessed, he bit down on her neck.

Ana's whole body stiffened and then she screamed. Loud and shrill. Her pussy clamped down so hard, it hurt. His orgasm reignited and his dick felt like it was exploding. Winston released her neck as his eyes rolled back, he groaned so loudly his throat hurt. The spasms around his cock turned to flutters, he eased his thrusts until he stopped moving all together, careful to keep his weight off of Ana. He could taste her on his lips. Utter joy coursed through him.

Her eyes were closed. She was breathing deeply. He placed a kiss on her lips. She moaned, her eyes fluttered. Winston brushed the hair from her face.

"You okay?"

She made a noise of affirmation.

"Is your neck okay?" The bite had broken the skin as was required. Winston licked the wound. Ana moaned and she shivered.

"You killed me," she murmured. Her voice a bit slurred. "Too good." Her eyes were still closed.

"The sex will get even better."

Her lids cracked open just a little. "No way." She shook her head.

"Yeah, when you bite me back." He brushed another kiss on her lips. He chuckled. "Have a powernap and then we'd better get back to the ceremony."

Her eyes widened but they were hazy. "Oh… oh flip."

"Sleep for a few minutes," he urged. "We haven't been gone that long."

"I want to do that again." She gave him a drunk looking smile.

"Later."

"Promise?" Her eyes were already closing. Her breathing deepening.

Winston chuckled. "I promise." Easiest promise he had ever made.

CHAPTER 26

ONE WEEK LATER...

They walked in silence, a group of six, all spread out. It was only he and Ash who walked side by side. They were on their way back to the village. They'd just shifted back into their human form. In a mile or two they'd be able to see the smoke. It was early yet, almost everyone would be sleeping.

"I can't believe you left your new mate to come on security detail. You must be desperate to get back to Ana." Ash glanced his way. "You're lucky I'm on this assignment or I would've kept her warm for you." He winked, making his meaning clear. *Fucker!*

"Don't even go there," Winston growled, even though the edges of his mouth were curled in a smile. He knew that his friend was messing with him. "We all have a role to play in keeping our village safe. I'm not going to shirk responsibility. Besides, we'd been holed up for a week. I left my female unconscious. I'm sure she's slept for two days solid. She needed the break."

Ash smirked. It made him look feral, something from a nightmare. "I'm sure I could've roused her."

"Fuck you, dickhead," Winston chuckled.

His friend did too. "So…" Ash turned serious. He lowered his voice since the other males were close. Not that anyone was particularly interested in what they were saying to one another. "Is it everything you thought it would be?"

"What, being mated?"

Ash nodded. "You look happy." His face became pinched, his eyes dark. Winston was sure he saw longing there. Was it longing for his lost mate or longing for real companionship? Probably both.

"It's everything and more," Winston's voice was thick with emotion as his mind moved to his female. He stopped walking. He could hear the footfalls of the others continuing ahead. The pine needles crunching beneath their feet.

"Yes," his friend sighed. "It's a gift and a curse."

Ash turned. Winston touched his friend on the arm. "I wish you would consider…"

"Nah, fuck…" He ran a hand through his hair, which was already an unruly mess. "I had a mate and I lost her… lost so much…" He shook his head. "I have my son, my pack. I'm happy. Very fucking happy."

"I hear you've been sniffing around the same female. Are you sure you—"

"The best fuck I ever had," Ash interjected. He looked angry. "That's all it is."

Winston choked out a laugh. "Seriously? Here I was thinking that you might be ready to—"

"Don't you dare say it."

"You and Ana have so much in common. She knows

what you are going through. That's why you guys get along so well."

"She's easy on the eyes and knows how to cook a steak. What's not to like?"

Winston couldn't help the growl that escaped. "Stop with the bullshit comments. Ana has had a difficult time and yet she was able to move on. It doesn't mean she forgot her mate or the child she lost—"

"Enough," Ash snarled. "I will never take another mate. Never! I may have spent the last few Shifter Nights with the same female but it doesn't mean a thing. In fact, I'm done with her."

"Look, it's your life." Winston put up both hands. "You need to decide for—"

One of the males growled. Winston's hackles went up.

"Look at this!" he yelled.

"What the fuck?" one of the others snarled.

He and Ash ran over to where the males were. They were looking at the ground.

"What the hell!" Winston mumbled. "What the fuck is that?" he added.

Ash leaned in close, he sniffed. "Nothing. I get nothing." The male scouted the area. "Nobody move." He scratched his head and sighed. "That's it. One fucking print."

"It's huge." Winston said. "What the hell made it?"

"Fucked if I know." Ash shook his head.

"It's like nothing I've ever seen before." Kane cocked his head, still staring at the print. "Bigger than a bear's but more like a… fuck… like a cat. Look at the claws and the pads of the paw. That's feline for sure."

"There's only one," Cody snarled, looking around them. "How is that possible?"

"We're only two miles from our village," Ash spoke low.

Winston shifted. It took him less than a second. Adrenaline coursed through him. His fur bristled.

"Try to stay calm." Ash looked him in the eyes. "Whatever made this is long gone. You can see how the wind has blown the edge. A leaf is lying in the center. I'd say at least," he pursed his lips in thought, "four, maybe five hours. I don't scent blood or…" he let the sentence die when Winston growled. "Let's head back. I need to speak with the alphas."

Blinding fear iced his veins. So much so that he was struggling to concentrate on what Ash was saying.

"You can go back to your mate." *Thank fuck!* Winston howled as his claws dug up the earth. He ran at a flat-out pace to the village, shifting as he made it to their front door.

Winston barged in, slammed the door behind him and dug himself under the covers, wrapping his arms around Ana.

His mate made a noise of contentment. "You're freezing." Her voice was laced with sleep.

"We might need to put our baby-making efforts on hold," he blurted, adrenaline still coursing through him.

She turned to face him, a frown marred her beautiful face. "It might be too late for that."

His heart beat faster. "Are you saying?" He frowned. "Are you…?"

"I'm not sure but my breasts feel a little tender and I was sick yesterday. I… maybe… Are you saying you don't want to be a dad anymore?"

Winston felt his eyes prick. "I'd like nothing more. I'm worried though." He told Ana what had happened.

"It could be anything. A bear?"

"It was one of them. It was one of the things that hurt Ward. The same fuckers that are scaring our game. It was right here... just outside our village." He pulled Ana close. His chest rising and falling quickly. Adrenaline spiked once again.

"Breathe," Ana kept her voice low. "In through your nose and out through your mouth. Slower... that's it."

Winston chuckled. "How the tables have turned." He pulled back, kissing her softly. "Do you want to know? I'm bursting to find out."

"Find out what?" She frowned, looking adorable.

"If you're with child."

Ana's eyes widened. "Would you be able to tell? It's too soon. I don't think I'd be more than a couple of days – a week at the most."

"I might." He smiled. "A week is a long time for a shifter baby."

Ana nodded. "I would really like to know."

Winston pulled the covers away exposing every inch of her beautiful body. He slowly moved down her until his nose was in line with her belly. It was flat and smooth. He buried his nose against her and sniffed, then he put his ear against her skin.

It was so soft he almost missed it. The tiniest pitter patter. He laughed. "You're right, it's too late." Then he sobered up a whole hell of a lot. He gathered Ana into his arms. "I'm going to take good care of you. I won't let you out of my sight."

Ana was smiling. "I take it I'm..." She chewed on her lower lip. A tear rolled down her cheek. "I'm pregnant."

"Yeah, sweetheart, you're going to be a mom. A fucking amazing, beautiful... sexy mom." He touched her belly. "I can't wait until you swell with child. Until your breasts fill with milk." He suckled on one.

She hugged him back.

"You have nothing to worry about." He couldn't keep the growl from his voice.

"Who said I was worried? I'm not. You will protect us. I feel completely safe with you, my love."

Winston had to work on keeping his breathing even. To keep from panicking. There was something out there. If he was right, there was more than one. They were big and they posed a threat. He growled low in his throat.

"Stop that," Ana giggled. "Your heart is just about beating out of your chest. I think," she wrapped her legs around his waist, "that you should make love to me. Pregnant women are exceedingly horny." She fisted his dick and, despite his raging fear, it hardened in her hand. "It'll take your mind off of things."

Winston nodded. "I can think of nothing better, mate… soon-to-be mother of my child." He grinned.

"I love the sound of that, and I love you." She sank onto him.

Winston kissed his female, trying hard to concentrate on bringing her pleasure instead of the terrible possibilities that ran through his mind. Each one worse than the last.

AUTHOR'S NOTE

This is the first in a three book series, so I won't leave you hanging for too long. Hope you enjoyed it.

A big thank you to my entire team, from my fabulous editors and cover designer, to my ARC readers. And then, of course, a big thank you to my readers. These books would not be possible without your loyal support.

If you want to be kept updated on new releases please sign up to my Latest Release Newsletter to ensure that you don't miss out http://mad.ly/signups/96708/join. I promise not to spam you or divulge your email address to a third party. I send my mailing list an exclusive sneak peek prior to release. All new sign-ups also receive a free novella — One Night with a Shifter.

I live on an acre in the country with my gorgeous husband and three sons and an array of pets. You can usually find me on the computer, completely lost in worlds of my making. I believe that it is the small things that truly matter like that feeling you get when you start a new book or a particularly beautiful sunset.

BOOKS BY THIS AUTHOR

The Chosen Series:
Book 1 ~ Chosen by the Vampire Kings
Book 2 ~ Stolen by the Alpha Wolf
Book 3 ~ Unlikely Mates
Book 4 ~ Awakened by the Vampire Prince
Book 5 ~ Mated to the Vampire Kings (Short Novel)
Book 6 ~ Wolf Whisperer (Novella)
Book 7 ~ Wanted by the Elven King

Demon Chaser Series (No cliffhangers):
Book 1 ~ Omega
Book 2 ~ Alpha
Book 3 ~ Hybrid
Book 4 ~ Skin
Demon Chaser Boxed Set Book 1–3

BOOKS BY THIS AUTHOR

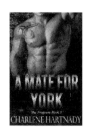

The Program Series (Vampire Novels):
Book 1 ~ A Mate for York
Book 2 ~ A Mate for Gideon
Book 3 ~ A Mate for Lazarus
Book 4 ~ A Mate for Griffin
Book 5 ~ A Mate for Lance
Book 6 ~ A Mate for Kai
Book 7 ~ A Mate for Titan

The Bride Hunt Series (Dragon Shifter Novels):
Book 1 ~ Royal Dragon
Book 2 ~ Water Dragon
Book 3 ~ Dragon King
Book 4 ~ Lightning Dragon
Book 5 ~ Forbidden Dragon
Book 6 ~ Dragon Prince

Excerpt

A MATE FOR YORK

The Program Book 1

CHARLENE HARTNADY

1

CASSIDY'S HANDS WERE CLAMMY and shaking. She had just retyped the same thing three times. At this rate, she would have to work even later than normal to get her work done. She sighed heavily.

Pull yourself together.

With shaking hands, she grabbed her purse from the floor next to her, reached inside and pulled out the folded up newspaper article.

Have you ever wanted to date a vampire?

Human women required. Must be enthusiastic about interactions with vampires. Must be willing to undergo a stringent medical exam. Must be prepared to sign a contractual agreement which would include a non-

disclosure clause. This will be a temporary position. Limited spaces available within the program. Successful candidates can earn up to $45,000 per day, over a three-day period.

All she needed was three days leave.

Cassidy wasn't sure whether her hands were shaking because she had to ask for the leave and her boss was a total douche bag or because the thought of vampires drinking her blood wasn't exactly a welcome one.

More than likely a combination of both.

This was a major opportunity for her though. She had already been accepted into the trial phase of the program that the vampires were running. What was three days in her life? So there was a little risk involved. Okay, a lot of risk, but it would all be worth it in the end. She was drowning in debt. Stuck in a dead-end job. Stuck in this godforsaken town. This was her chance, her golden opportunity, and she planned on seizing it with both hands.

To remind herself what she was working towards, or at least running away from, she let her eyes roam around her cluttered desk. There were several piles of documents needing to be filed. A stack of orders lay next to her cranky old laptop. Hopefully it wouldn't freeze on her this time while she was uploading them into the system. It had been months since Sarah had left. There used to be two of them performing her job, and since her colleague was never replaced it was just her. She increasingly found that she had to get to work way earlier and stay later and later just to get the job done.

To add insult to injury, there were many days that her a-hole boss still had the audacity to come down on her for not meeting a deadline. He refused to listen to reason and would not accept being understaffed as an excuse. She'd never been one to shy away from hard work but the expectations were ridiculous. Her only saving grace was that she didn't have much of a life.

There had to be something more out there for her – and a hundred and thirty-five thousand big ones would not only pay off her debts but would also give her enough cash to go out and find one. A life, that is, and a damned good life it would be.

Cassidy took a deep breath and squared her shoulders. If she asked really nicely, hopefully Mark would give her a couple of days off. She couldn't remember the last time she had taken leave. Then it dawned on her, she'd taken three days after Sean had died a year ago. Her boss couldn't say no though. If he did, she wasn't beyond begging.

Rising to her feet, she made for the closed door at the other end of her office. After knocking twice, she entered.

The lazy ass was spread out on the corner sofa with his hands crossed behind his head. He didn't look in the least bit embarrassed about her finding him like that either.

"Cassidy." He put on a big cheesy smile as he rose to a sitting position. The buttons on his jacket pulled tight around his paunchy midsection. He didn't move much and ate big greasy lunches so it wasn't surprising. "Come on in. Take a seat," he gestured to a spot next to him on the sofa.

That would be the day. Her boss could get a bit touchy feely. Thankfully it had never gone beyond a pat on the butt, a hand on her shoulder or just a general invasion of her personal space. It put her on edge though because it was becoming worse of late. The sexual innuendos were also getting highly irritating. She pretended that they went over her head, but he was becoming more and more forward as time went by.

By the way his eyes moved down her body, she could tell that he was most definitely mentally undressing her. *Oh god.* That meant that he was in one of his grabby moods. *Damn.* She preferred it when he was acting like a total jerk. Easier to deal with.

"No, that's fine. Thank you." She worked hard to plaster a smile on her face. "I don't want to take up much of your time and I have to get back to work myself."

His eyes narrowed for a second before dropping to her breasts. "You could do with a little break every now and then... so could I for that matter." Even though she knew he couldn't see anything because of her baggy jacket, his eyes stayed glued to her boobs anyway. Why did she get the distinct impression that he was no longer talking about work? *Argh!*

"How long has your husband been gone now?" he asked, his gaze still locked on her chest. It made her want to fold her arms but she resisted the temptation.

None of your damned business.

"It's been a year now since Sean passed." She tried hard to look sad and mournful. The truth was, if the bastard wasn't already dead she would've killed him herself. Turned out that there were things about Sean that she hadn't known. In fact, it was safe to say that she'd been living with and married to a total stranger. Funny how those things tended to come out when a person died.

Her boss did not need to know this information though. So far, playing the mourning wife was the only thing that kept him from pursuing her further.

"What can I do for you?" His eyes slid down to the juncture at her thighs and she had to fight the urge to squeeze them tightly together. Even though temperatures outside were damn near scorching, she still wore stockings, skirt to mid-calf, a button-up blouse and a jacket. Nothing was revealing and yet he still looked at her like she was standing there naked. It made her skin crawl. "I would be happy to oblige you. Just say the word, baby."

She hated it when he called her that. He started doing it a couple of weeks ago. Cassidy had asked him on several occasions to stop but she may as well have been speaking to a plank of wood.

She grit her teeth for a second, holding back a retort. "Great. Glad to hear it." Her voice sounded way more confident than she felt. "I need a couple of days off. It's been a really long time —"

"Forget it," he interrupted while standing up. "I need you... here." Another innuendo. Although she waited, he didn't give any further explanations.

"Look, I know there is a lot to do around here especially since Sarah left." His eyes clouded over immediately at the mention of her ex-colleague's name. "I would be happy to put in extra time."

As in, she wouldn't sleep and would have to work weekends to get the job done.

"I'll do whatever it takes. I just really need a couple of days. It's important."

His eyes lit up and she realized what she had just said and how it would've sounded to a complete pig like Mark.

"Anything?" he rolled the word off of his tongue.

"Well..." It came out sounding breathless but only

because she was nervous. "Not anything. What I meant to say was —"

"No, no. I like that you would do anything, in fact, there is something I've been meaning to discuss with you." His gaze dropped to her breasts again.

Please no. Anything but that.

Cassidy swallowed hard, actually feeling sick to her stomach. She shook her head.

"You can have a few days, baby. In fact, I'll hire you an assistant." Ironically he played with the wedding band on his ring finger. His voice had turned sickly sweet. "I'd be willing to go a long way for you if you only met me halfway. It's time you got over the loss of your husband and I plan on helping you to do that."

"Um… I don't think…" Her voice was soft and shaky. Her hands shook too, so she folded her arms.

This was not happening.

"Look, Cass… baby, you're an okay-looking woman. Not normally the type I'd go for. I prefer them a bit younger, bigger tits, tighter ass…" He looked her up and down as if he were sizing her up and finding her lacking. "I'd be willing to give you a go… help you out. Now… baby…" he paused.

Cassidy felt like the air had seized in her lungs, like her heart had stopped beating. Her mouth gaped open but she couldn't close it. She tried to speak but could only manage a croak.

She watched in horror as her boss pulled down his zipper and pulled out a wrinkled, flaccid cock. "Suck on this. Or you could bend over and I'll fuck you – the choice is yours. I would recommend the fuck because quite frankly I think you could use it." He was deadly serious. Even gave a small nod like he was doing her a favor or something.

To the delight of her oxygen starved lungs, she managed to suck in a deep breath but still couldn't get any words out. Not a single, solitary syllable.

"I know you've had to play the part of the devastated wife and all that but I'm sure you really want a bit of this." He waved his cock at her, although wave was not the right description. The problem was that a limp dick couldn't really wave. It flopped about pathetically in his hand.

Cassidy looked from his tiny dick up to his ruddy, pasty face and back down again before bursting out laughing. It was the kind of laugh that had her bending at the knees, hunching over. Sucking in another lungful of air, she gave it all she had. Unable to stop even if she wanted to. Until tears rolled down her cheeks. Until she was gasping for breath.

"Hey now…" Mark started to look distinctly uncomfortable. "That's not really the sort of response I expected from you." He didn't look so sure anymore, even started to put his dick away before his eyes hardened.

Cassidy wiped the tears from her face. She still couldn't believe what the hell she was seeing and even worse, what she was hearing. *What a complete asshole.*

Her boss took a step towards her. "The time for games is over. Get down on your knees if you want to keep your job. I'm your boss and your behavior is just plain rude."

Any hint of humor evaporated in an instant. "I'll tell you what's rude… you taking out your thing is rude. You're right, you're my boss which means what is happening right here," she gestured between the two of them, looking pointedly at his member, "is called sexual harassment."

He narrowed his eyes at her. "Damn fucking straight, little missy. I want you to sexually harass this right now." He clutched his penis, flopping it around some more.

"Alrighty then. Let me just go and fetch my purse," she grinned at him, putting every little bit of sarcasm she had into the smile.

"Why would you need your purse?" he frowned.

"To get my magnifying glass. You have just about the smallest dick that I've ever seen." Not that she had seen many, but she didn't think she needed to. His penis was a joke.

It was his turn to gape. To turn a shade of bright red. "You didn't just say that. I'm going to pretend that I didn't hear that. This is your last fucking chance." Spittle flew from his mouth. "Show me your tits and get onto your fucking knees. Make me fucking come and do it now or you are out of a job."

"You can pretend all you want. As far as I'm concerned you can pretend that I'm sucking on your limp dick as well, because it will never happen. You can take your job and your tiny penis and shove um where the sun don't shine!" Cassidy almost wanted to slap a hand over her mouth, she couldn't believe that she had just said all of that. One thing was for sure, she was done taking shit from men. *Done!*

She gave him a disgusted look, turned on her heel and walked out. After grabbing her purse, she left without looking back, praying that her old faithful car would start. It hadn't been serviced since before her husband had died and it wasn't sounding right lately. The gearbox grated sometimes when she changed gears. There was a rattling noise. She just didn't have the funds. That was all about to change though. She hadn't exactly planned on leaving her job just yet. What if things didn't work out? She'd planned on keeping her job as a safety net instead of counting chickens she didn't have. It was too late to go back now.

Despite her lack of a backup plan, Cassidy grinned as her car started with a rattle and a splutter. Grinned even wider as she pulled away, hearing the gravel crunch beneath her tires. Now all she had to do was get through the next few days and she was home free.

A Mate for York is available now.

Printed in Great Britain
by Amazon